THE MUSIC MASTER

LINDY GRAHAM

First Published in Great Britain by Crystal Clear Books 2024

Copyright © Linda Parkinson-Hardman, 2024

Linda Parkinson-Hardman has asserted her right under the Copyright Design and Patents Act 1988 to be identified as the author of this work.

This book is a work of fiction and, except in the case of historial fact, any resemblences to actual persons, living or dead, is purely coincidental.

No paragraph of this publication may be reproduced, copied or transmitted save with written permission or in accordance with the provisions of the Copyright, Designs and Patents Act 1988, or under the terms of any license, permitting limited copying issued by the Copyright Licensing Agency, 33 Alfred Place, London, WC1E 7DP.

Published by: Crystal Clear Books

ISBN: 978-1-7394272-4-5

Cover Image: Photo 45202122 | Puppet Master © Tijanap | Dreamstime.com

For Stevie, Pip and Belle

These are the pieces of my youth, the small secrets and the not-so-great expectations that defined my coming of age.

Daniel Armand Lee

OVERTURE

Our runner handed me the box.

'This was delivered for you Jenny'

This was the bit I always dreaded. I knew the other members of Raptio all felt the same. I imagined them standing just behind their dressing room door with a box in their hands as the years melted away, again.

Sally's rose would be yellow and the note would say 'my sweetest one'. Marianne's pink, with a note that said 'my beautiful girl'; Laura's is always the deepest red and the note it contains tells her she is 'my perfect rose'. And mine? Mine is black, the only one without a natural colour, and the note always says 'My beloved'. I didn't have to open the box to look inside, it was the same every time.

I felt sick, a common reaction to the same event that had been a feature of our lives for so many years. Thrusting the box in the bin I called out.

'Jamie, it's arrived.'

'Good, it's begun.' His face was impassive.

He hugged me, kissing me gently on my forehead. 'Knock 'em dead kiddo.' It was our joke, said for luck as much as anything else.

CHAPTER ONE

'Now you Jenny.'

Rolling my eyes at Victoria and Diane I lifted the violin to my chin and without thought, bowed a perfect C sharp for the first time in a year of practice.

The effect was cataclysmic; a tidal wave hit me in the tummy and ended between my legs. I felt my chest flush as my face turned beetroot. I must have gasped as the whole of 3B turned to stare at me.

'Are you feeling alright Jenny?' Miss Brough was solicitous.

Not trusting myself to speak I nodded croaking, 'Period'. Embarrassed, she looked away waving me out of the room.

I felt my friends and classmates' stares piercing my shoulder blades as I dumped the violin on the desk and rushed for the door.

In the corridor, I leant my head against the cool cream brickwork waiting for my heart to stop hammering and my breath to slow down. I could feel a pulsing warm glow between my legs and with no idea about what had just happened, I headed for the loo.

Pulling down my knickers I checked for blood. My period wasn't due, there had been none of the usual cramps or sicky feeling that normally heralded its onset. My fingers probed between my legs, it was hot, tender and very wet. I pulled them away sharply and checked, no blood. A smell, musty and with the faint odour of fish rose from my hand and, wrinkling my nose I wiped it on some loo paper.

As I sat quietly wondering what had just happened the heat in my face and chest subsided, my heart slowed, and my stomach stopped doing back flips.

I thought back over the hushed conversations about sex with friends. Instinctively I knew it was related but had no idea how or why. Our limited knowledge was of practising kisses on the backs of our hands and watching teachers put condoms on bananas in biology.

I touched myself again, all that was left was a slight tingle and I shivered.

The school lunch bell rang. I'd sat in the cubicle longer than I thought. Wiping myself dry with the scratchy loo paper I pulled up my damp knickers, they felt uncomfortable and I was sure everyone would know, would smell the odour that drifted upwards. I washed my hands thoroughly but to me the smell just lingered longer.

My best friends were already at our table when I arrived.

'What happened to you then?' Victoria, the nosiest of my friends, demanded.

I rolled my eyes, 'just my period'.

Victoria was having none of it. 'Really?' she looked sceptical, 'That was a very noisy period, and you went scarlet …'

Diane leaned over and touched my hand, 'Ignore her, she's just annoyed that you managed a perfect C sharp, Miss Brough was full of it after you'd left'.

'Phh', Victoria waved her hand, 'I don't think I've ever heard a perfect note from any of our instruments before.' She smiled at me and the inquisition, such as it was, passed over.

That night in my room preparing for an evening of scales and exam music I wondered if the same thing would happen. Tentatively I picked up my violin and tried another C sharp ... nothing. I started scales practice and quickly engrossed I began varying speed and intensity. Nothing happened and after an hour of feeling oddly disappointed, I headed downstairs to supper with my parents.

I put the day's events out of my head and after I was released from the dining table I began my practice in earnest. Lifting the violin again I bowed another single, perfect C sharp. The note resonated with my inner tuning fork and snaked its way down my spine until hit the sweet spot and a beautiful, amazing, glorious cascade of tingly experiences flooded my body. It felt like a forest full of fairy lights was twinkling away inside me, and without the constraint of other people watching, I was able to let it run its course, enjoying the ride.

When it subsided for a second time I wondered if the effect would be matched by any other notes. I tried an A sharp, but the effect although discernable was much less pronounced. Slowly I worked my way through the scales, working hard to get into the correct position to achieve the elusive perfect note, testing each one until I found those that made my body sing the strongest and longest. It was a revelation that would, in time become a curse.

Lunchtime the following day found me in the school library trying to find anything to explain what was happening. I started in the biology section, looking up 'reproduction', but all I found were a couple of kids' picture books that told me nothing I didn't already know. In hushed tones, I asked the duty librarian if there was anything about sex available but she looked at me blankly before giving a categoric 'No.'

I wandered into our common room looking for any sort of distraction. I picked up a magazine discarded by someone else and leafed through, stopping on the letters page when a word I didn't know jumped out.

'Have you read this?' I looked at Diane, holding out the copy of Jackie.

'Mmmmmm' she mumbled, not paying attention.

Holding it under her nose I pointed at the letters page.

'Yes of course I have – Mummy bought it last week, I left it there for the others to read if they wanted.' She pushed it away from me to focus on what she was reading.

'Dear Cathy and Claire,' I started reading aloud,

She looked up, 'Why are you so interested in Cathy and Claire suddenly?'.

I shrugged, 'I dunno, it was different from the usual, you know.'

Diane looked at me curiously, her eyes narrowed. 'Different, how different?'

'Well, you know, more ..' I struggled to find the words '... informative' I finished lamely.

Snorting back a laugh she turned back to her magazine.

I rolled the word around in my head, 'orgasm'. It sounded like a combination of exotic and arousal, and I only had to think about it to get a fleeting, tingly reminder of the effect the notes had had on my body just the night before.

At home, I started practising even harder. Where music had been a source of solitary companionship, keeping me company in the long evenings between school days now I found it moved me physically as well as emotionally.

I begged my parents for my own record player and invested weeks of pocket money in all the great composers and performers. Out went Donny and Marie and in came Paganini, Puccini and Maria Callas. If they were surprised at my sudden turnaround they didn't say anything, simply allowing me to play my records more loudly than I'd been able to before.

At school, music class and personal practice became a series of lessons in self-control. Miss Brough was disparaging when for the sixth time in a row, I failed to strike the right balance between note and score.

'Jenny, I really don't know what's come over you,' she sighed, 'one minute you play as if you were a member of an elite orchestra and the next, you're a beginner, please, please keep to what's in the score.'

I would mumble yet another apology and raise my violin to my chin to try again.

By the end of my third year at Jamiesons, I was able to contain the most visible effect some pieces had on me. I understood more about those that worked with my body and those that didn't. If I wanted an easy time in class or practice, I would ask for the latter. If I was feeling adventurous then I'd go with the former. I improved immeasurably and my parents started conversations with Miss Brough in earnest about a career in music, making sure it was given top priority when I chose the 'O' levels I'd be sitting at the end of my fifth year.

CHAPTER TWO

Hugh checked his reflection in the rear-view mirror, climbed out of his sports car and took in the façade with its striking Doric columns. He'd pulled up right outside the school, even though it had been an express instruction not to do so in the agency's letter of recommendation.

Grabbing his briefcase, he walked up the short flight of steps and into a grand, high-ceilinged entrance hall. A desk on the right pointed to Reception so following the implied instruction, he opened the door indicated. The other side of the door was clearly school territory. Unlike the beautiful entrance hall designed to impress visitors in ages past, this corridor showed the scuff marks and faded paint of years of rough handling. He imagined hundreds of girls flinging down hockey and lacrosse sticks, running their hands along the walls or standing sullenly waiting for judgment.

This will do very nicely he thought.

He knocked on the door marked Reception and pushed it open. A young woman sat at a desk opposite.

She smiled. 'You must be Mr Smithson, welcome to Jamieson's.'

He nodded. 'Nice to meet you …?'

'Alison', she offered, standing up and holding out her hand.

'Alison.' He repeated, taking her hand and shaking it firmly. 'Is there anywhere I can get a cup of tea it's been a long drive?', he smiled.

'Of course, take a seat and I'll go and get you one before I let Miss Dickson know you've arrived. Milk and sugar?'

'Milk and one please.' He sat where indicated while she left the room.

Looking around he spotted the usual paraphernalia of a busy school office. Timetables tacked to noticeboards, filing cabinets covered with paperwork and folders, hand-made calendars and cards probably made by students on behalf of grateful parents, and the required dying plant on the window sill. It was stuffy and stuffed, and smelt of chalk dust and cabbage.

'Someone really ought to open a window', he thought before turning his attention to the returning Alison who had arrived with a steaming mug in her hand.

'I assumed you'd like a mug,' she explained looking him over. 'You don't look like the teacup type'. She smiled, and her face dimpled prettily.

Hugh surreptitiously gave her left hand a swift glance, the ring finger showed no evidence of engagement or marriage.

'I'll let Miss Dickson know you're here.' Alison turned left and out of view again.

Hugh smiled and sat back cupping the hot mug in his cold hands; thank God James had done what he'd asked and given him a good reference.

Alison popped her head around the door. 'Miss Dickson will see you now Mr Smithson' and held out her hand for the now empty mug.

Miss Dickson was not as he expected. Headmistresses of girls' schools were usually robust creatures echoing a bygone Enid Blyton era of jolly hockey sticks and cold showers. This one, by contrast, was younger and looked more intelligent than most. He noticed the sign on her desk, Dr Dickson, and he gave her his most winning smile.

'Mr Smithson', I'm so pleased to meet you.' Standing, Emma Dickson offered him her hand and then indicated he should sit down. 'What a stroke of luck you were available at such short notice. As you know from the agency, Ms Geeson, our primary German teacher is pregnant and having a rather difficult time of it by all accounts, so she has left us early.'

'I just happened to be between posts, family business you know.' he demurred, 'and this suited my needs now that it's all been sorted out.'

'I understand from the agency you teach German up to A level, is that correct?'

He understood Miss Dickson was planning to get her money's worth out of him.

'Yes, that's right. I'm fluent and can even coach for university entrance exams if that might be useful.' He used the salesman's trick of over-delivering to gain a few extra Brownie points.

'Excellent, excellent that sounds like a jolly good idea.' She looked at him thoughtfully. 'The letter also says you are a pianist able to support students as an accompanist?'. She moved forward a little in her chair and he rightly intuited she needed a pianist.

'Yes, that's also true. I had hoped to study music professionally while I was in Germany, but sadly I didn't have the requisite talent or gift. Now I play only for personal pleasure.' He smiled at her again.

'Well, that's just marvellous. We have so many girls studying music these days and Miss Brough our music teacher can't keep up and is feeling the pressure. It would be helpful to have someone who can take over some of the accompanist work with the older pupils in particular.'

'I'm not a music teacher as such but I can help those who are already well along their musical journeys to understand how to express themselves through music. It was something I was particularly good at when I was studying myself.' His hands moved in fluent circular gestures as he spoke, almost in time to the rhythm of the words, as if to emphasise the point.

The headmistress smiled. 'I think we'll get along very nicely Mr Smithson, you sound perfect for our needs and the letter of reference from James Masterson spoke very highly of you. As such, I'd be very pleased if you were to consider taking us on this coming academic year, starting on Monday if that suits?'

The question was apparent in the upward lilt of her voice, and he answered positively.

'Yes, that would suit me very well indeed Miss Dickson, and thank you I'm looking forward to working at such a prestigious school'. He stood and offered his hand which she grasped firmly in turn, shaking it once.

The interview had come to an end.

'Oh, just one thing Mr Smithson'. She smiled. 'Please don't park in front of the school building again, you were informed by the agency that the teacher's car park is at the rear past the tennis courts it sets such a poor example when the staff don't pay attention to the rules.'

'Of course, I'm sorry, I forgot.' He lied smoothly. 'It won't happen again Miss Dickson.'

CHAPTER THREE

Mr Smithson joined the school's teaching staff at the beginning of my fourth year. Old by teenagers' standards, with a look that spoke of dire consequences for those misbehaving on his watch. He ignored the favoured slacks, shirt, sports jacket and tie of our male teachers in favour of jeans and tightly stretched black polo neck jumpers. He smelt of coffee, smoke and Habit Rouge, the fragrance my father used on nights out. He was not something our all-girls school was used to.

In a very short space of time, it seemed, he had an adoring army of young girls who surrounded him at every opportunity.

'Mr Smithson are you married?' they would ask, hoping he might glance in their direction, just the once.

'Mr Smithson, are you going to the school disco?' Hoping the answer would be yes, and he would risk his position with a single dance to a slow track.

His answers, from what I knew based on conversations with Victoria and Diane, were always functional, giving nothing away about the inner man, or what he thought of the attention he attracted. Occasionally it seemed, he played along saying 'yes' to the school disco questions and then, in the evening, spending all his time chatting with the oldest of the female teachers, paying them the attention even the youngest girls craved.

I watched from the sidelines as I wasn't taking German so never had reason to come across him except like passing ships in the corridors. I was curious about what they all saw in him but as I was self-sufficient in my music, I did not need any passion other than that contained in my violin case.

It was only years later I understood that it must have been the combination of my musical passion and significant disinterest that had registered with him. A heady mix for someone used to being adored by every young girl crossing his path.

'Isn't he gorgeous?' Victoria sighed, staring at the teacher's table in the dining hall.

Rolling my eyes at Diane. 'I don't know what you see in him, either of you'.

Diane laughed. 'You've got nothing in your head except your music these days Jenny.'

'You really can't see it can you?' Victoria was curious.

I just shook my head. 'No, not really. I mean I can see he is good-looking, but ...' I stopped and stared at him until he, feeling the strength of my gaze looked back at me. Turning away quickly '.. he's not my type.' I finished in a rush.

Victoria was scathing. 'Not your type? How do you know what your type is? The only boys you fancy are all long-dead 'musicians' as you call them. To emphasise the point she made two hand quotes around the word musicians.

'He's starting a music discussion group with Miss Brough, I heard them talking about it in the corridor.' Diane spoke quietly so the others on our table didn't hear as it was considered bad form to listen in on other people's conversations.

'Really, I thought he taught German.' Victoria perked up. 'I think I might just join.'

I couldn't help laughing. 'You would Victoria. You fancy the pants off him but he's never going to look at kids like us. And anyway, he's dating Alison.'

'I know and it pains me to admit that the school secretary has more allure than I do.' Victoria dramatically held one hand to her heart and swept the other back across her brow.

We all laughed, never imagining for a minute what might happen in the future.

The year hadn't long started when I found him sitting in the music room instead of Miss Brough when I turned up for my weekly practice.

'Don't worry, I may teach German, but I also play the piano passably well, at least well enough to accompany you.' He smiled at me encouragingly. 'Miss Bough isn't well and Miss Dickson asked me to sit in. Is that OK with you?'

I nodded accepting his explanation, relieved I had a choice.

Removing my violin from its case I raised it to my chin with a sigh. I was preparing Vivaldi's Violin Concerto in A Minor for a forthcoming recital in town and although I was nervous my mind was on the music. Relaxing, I allowed myself to be carried along by the slow, delicate story. Reaching the high my body arched with the notes; delving deep into the lows my body stilled its search for ecstasy and drifted with the thematics.

By the time I had finished the first movement, I was on the cliff's edge. I tipped over with Pachelbel's 'Canon in D', barely containing myself in the crescendo. I could feel my hands shaking on the bow as I brought my body under control, the violin perched underneath my chin twitched at the internal spasms and I skipped and jumped over notes and phrases that were usually second nature to me.

Mr Smithson had prepared well, accompanying me intelligently and allowing me to make my own mistakes and decisions about emphasis and phrasing. It was something Miss Brough never did. She was forever on at me about how to do it her way rather than letting me find my own expression. By the time my hour's lesson was at an end, I'd accepted him as a suitable substitute.

Afterwards, he walked with me to the school gate. And when he held his hand out it took me a moment to realise, he wanted me to shake it. I barely touched the outstretched hand, a limp grasp was all I could manage.

'It's nice to meet you, Jennifer.' He said using my full name and grasping my hand firmly before turning away to walk to the teachers' car park. I stood for a moment, off-kilter and left mystified by such an unusual interaction between a teacher and child. I mulled it over all the way home, trying to work out what it all meant concluding I was reading too much into it.

Throwing my bag down in the boot room as soon as I was in I phoned Victoria, 'You'll never guess what just happened?'

'You're right, I'll never guess what just happened Jenny so why don't you just tell me'.

She was obviously in the middle of something.

'Mr Smithson …'. I let the words hang in the air knowing it would get her attention.

'Mr Smithson what?' she demanded.

'Well, he's just taken my music practice as Miss Brough had to go home early.'

'No … you're joking, aren't you?'

'And he shook my hand at the school gate and said it was nice to meet me too …'. I let that one sink in for a few minutes before adding, 'What do you think of that then?'

She let out a long whistle. 'Well, what a dark horse you are Jennifer Hunter. I didn't think you liked him?'

'I don't, I just thought it was a strange thing to do.' I thought about it, 'I don't think anyone's ever shaken my hand before, especially not an adult and someone I don't know. It felt a bit too close, do you know what I mean?' I was anxious to know it wasn't just me who thought it was odd.

She laughed. 'Mmm, I think so too. I'll see you tomorrow, bright and early before the bell goes so we can talk about it with Diane'. And she put the phone down.

A week later I found myself in the doorway of the practice room, and once again Mr Smithson was sitting at the piano, waiting. This time I didn't question it and he offered no explanation. We just got on with my practice pieces.

The Canon in D was fine as it was. As a favourite, I played it constantly adding in what my father called folderols and fripperies. With no interruption from a teacher, I gave myself a little extra freedom from the strict confines of the manuscript, finding nuances I hadn't realised were there before.

The Vivaldi on the other hand needed a lot more work. Personal practice had not gone well at home as every time I started playing I was caught up in the memory of Mr Smithson smiling at me as he played along.

Once again at the end of practice he walked me to the school gate and shook my hand when we parted company, this time with a cheery, 'I'll see you next week Jenny', before disappearing leaving me even more mildly confused.

CHAPTER FOUR

The first Monday morning dawned bright and clear, and Hugh chose his look carefully. Not too conformist or too challenging either. A black polo neck and jeans he decided, was the right combination of smart and casual, and shouldn't cause too much offence in the staff room, this was the 1970s after all.

He dabbed a small amount of Habit Rouge over his shaved face and slicked back his hair. Not bad he thought, you don't look a day over 27. Smiling at the mirror he checked his teeth for stray food and cupping a hand over his mouth, sniffed, all was clear. Gathering up his briefcase and books he left for his first day at Jamieson's School for Girls.

His first class went well. The girls were fascinated by him. And, after checking out the competition in the staff room he could understand why. The other teachers were older even than his real age and dressed in the classic slacks, shirt, tie, and battered tweed jacket if they were male; and frumpy skirts and blouses if they were female. There wasn't a single member of the teaching staff he found remotely interesting, but he resolved to be pleasant and kind to them all.

The first few weeks passed uneventfully. He watched and waited, amused by the attention he received from the students. Hugh was good at ignoring their comments and Alison was more than happy to go to the cinema or out for the occasional meal. They kissed chastely at the end of each evening and shared smiles and glances when they passed each other in the corridor or the dining room.

His fan club, as Alison referred to it, followed him everywhere. It was fortunate he had taken rooms in the next town as they could have become a lot more troublesome.

At the first school disco shared jointly with the nearest boy's school, he spent the entire evening talking to Miss Dickson and Miss Brough. He had no intention of letting his guard down this early in the game.

There were a few pupils who interested him, who had what he considered 'potential. One had caught his attention, and although her friends were all members of the fan club, she was aloof and disinterested. She wasn't exactly rude, she always smiled or said hello if they passed in the corridor; instead, it was more as if she were completely self-contained, and didn't need anything outside herself.

His opportunity to meet her properly came when Miss Brough was unexpectedly taken ill, and he was instructed by Miss Dickson to take over her practice sessions for the week.

'Hello.' The girl looked around the practice room nervously. 'I was looking for Miss Brough.'

'Unfortunately, she's been taken ill and I've been asked to step in as a replacement, is that alright with you?' He smiled confidently adding, 'I do know how to play the piano to accompany you and I'm sure we'll muddle along.'

'Oh, ok.' She stared at him unsure what should happen next. 'Do you know my practice pieces?'

'Miss Brough told me you were doing a Vivaldi and the Canon in D. If that's right, then we'll be fine as Vivaldi is one of my favourite composers. Shall we give it a go?'

Reassured she nodded and took her violin out of its case to begin warming up. When she was ready, she looked at him and he began the opening bars of the Vivaldi.

The hour flew by. He was pleased to see her start to relax in his company. He had read the notes left by Miss Brough about Jenny and disregarded them. The girl had a gift, a natural talent and he was, he decided, the one to help it blossom. He knew he'd only be able to do that if she trusted him to let her find her way.

They left the school building together. Turning to her at the school gates he held out his hand. She was momentarily nonplussed not understanding what was expected of her. She was slow to reciprocate and her hand felt softly pliable in his.

'It's nice to meet you, Jenny.' And with that, he turned and walked off sure in the knowledge of the effect his formality would have. He was so pleased with himself that he even started humming a jaunty little sea shanty. It was as much as he could do to contain a skip to one side.

Hugh cornered Miss Brough in the staff room the following week.

'How are you feeling? Better I hope?'

She smiled thinly. 'Yes, much better thank you.' Although the blue rings around her eyes and the strain in her voice told a different story.

'I know how much time you give to pupil practice outside school hours and thought maybe I could help out, with one or two of the older ones perhaps who don't need so much actual tuition, and just need accompanying?' He endeavoured to fold his face into an expression of concern.

'Well, I don't know.' She was cautious, 'I mean it would be nice to have some extra time to myself. I would need to ask Miss Dickson and the parents for their permission.' Despite her words, she looked grateful.

He smiled at her. 'That's fine. Any time you think I can help just let me know. I'm not a great teacher like you but I can help pupils prepare for exams or concerts.'

The compliment worked its magic and Miss Brough touched his arm saying, 'It would be so nice to have someone to help who understands the importance of music', adding, 'I'll speak to Miss Dickson.'

Later that day he was summoned to Miss Dickson's office.

'I hear you offered help to Miss Brough.' She stated it as a fact.

'Yes, she sounded tired when I asked her how she was'. He hoped it sounded considerate and caring.

'Mmm.' Miss Dickson regarded him thoughtfully. 'She has been having rather a lot of migraines recently and has a lot of after-school classes. I remember you said that although you weren't a music teacher you could accompany so I think we'll start with two of the older girls, Jennifer Hunter, and Gillian Ashfordly. Both are preparing for public concerts. If you can take them on, I'm sure Miss Brough would be very grateful.'

Hugh could barely contain his delight it was exactly the outcome he'd hoped for with the two girls who interested him most.

'Of course, Miss Dickson and I will report to Miss Brough regularly so she can make sure both girls are performing to the required standard.' He was quick to make the offer of reporting after all, he didn't want anyone checking up on him.

'Well, I don't think there's anything else for the time being and I've informed both the girls' parents already, so you are free to begin with their next practice sessions. Miss Bough will let you know their timetables.'

He was dismissed.

As far as Hugh was concerned the day had ended well. Hot footing to the school office he asked Alison if she were free that evening and she, being very interested in him and hoping he was at least as interested in her, was. He arranged to collect her at seven for dinner at eight.

CHAPTER FIVE

Jenny was less surprised to see Mr Smithson in the practice room the second time. He knew she had enjoyed their first practice session because she'd said as much to Miss Bough who was less pleased than she might have been. Noses and joints sprang to mind when she diffidently passed him the compliment. He simply filed it away in the box in his head marked 'Jenny'.

Having been given free rein the previous week he wondered what Jenny might do this time and endeavoured to make the session as much about her own expression as the musical notation would allow for.

It was no surprise to him when she gave the same involuntary sigh on lifting the violin to her neck. He was sure she wasn't aware of it but the gambler in him always noticed the tells. He settled down to the role of accompanist, occasionally stopping her to make a few suggestions here and there, but otherwise leaving her to it.

While he played, he watched her carefully, his inner radar noticed all the little signals she gave off as the music called forth its emotional intensity. Seemingly, minor and insignificant gestures and looks that gave her game away. He could tell she was struggling to keep it under control and guessed she wasn't ready to share her growing sexuality with anyone just yet. He didn't mind he could wait.

Jenny finished the Pachelbel and looked at him. 'How was that?'

He liked that she was so straightforward. There was no dissembling, no need for anything other than the truth. 'It was good, there were a couple of parts that could do with some extra work.' He leaned over her to point them out on the score. 'Here and here, I think need practice and you could try just running them over and over into each other to get a better feel for them.'

She nodded, 'I thought so too. When you say run them over and over do you mean just keep repeating them?'

He nodded.

'Oh, ok I can try that when I practice next.' She hesitated 'Will it be you next time too?'.

He liked the fact she smiled broadly when he confirmed it would indeed be him rather than Miss Brough, taking her practice sessions from now on.

'Miss Brough has a lot on her plate with so many girls taking music. I think she is glad of the help I can give.' He explained.

And, after practice, they walked once again through the school to the gates and he shook her hand, catching her off balance a second time.

Several weeks passed. Each practice ended at the school gate with a formal goodnight.

It hadn't taken as long with Gillian who revealed herself within a couple of weeks, but other than a quick touch on her arm and leg to move her into a better playing position he resisted the urge and waited for Jenny to come to him herself. Self-sufficient, confident and a little sassy, he knew she would be the best pupil he'd ever had.

When she did show him the extent of her passion with another perfect C sharp, he knew it was time. He watched her back arch, a flush appearing above her school blouse and the involuntary widening of her stance to steady herself.

Jenny didn't appear to notice him watching her and brought it all quickly back under control, panting quietly as the tidal wave receded from her body.

'You enjoy music don't you Jenny?' Hugh asked the question guilelessly at the end of their practice. rather like someone might comment on a painting in a gallery. He didn't want to alarm her at this early stage, he just wanted her to acknowledge the impact music had on her and by inference, him.

'Yes.' She turned her head away embarrassed.

'Would you like to join me for a coffee Jenny?'

Hugh found the following weeks a delicious blend of anticipation and disappointment. After her mother had given her assent to coffee after school, he was careful to keep things above board, both for the school and the café they frequented. He wanted their union to be a natural progression of a relationship built on trust and music.

By Christmas, Hugh had effectively replaced Miss Brough as Jenny's music teacher. He accompanied her at the various concerts she was involved with over the holiday period. When the January term began, he suggested to her parents that more frequent practice sessions would be a good investment, increasing from once a week to twice a week. Jenny readily agreed to the new arrangements. In February her parents also agreed to extend each session from one to two hours.

He had explained it well. 'After all, when she goes to college, she'll be required to do formal practice for a dozen or more hours a week so she might as well get used to it now.' Her father even started calling her his 'little virtuoso'.

The tape recorder was an inspired idea. It meant that she got used to the idea so that when the time came, he'd be able to play their recordings and others wouldn't hear anything other than a piano accompanying violin if they happened to be listening carefully outside the mostly soundproof rooms.

Jenny agreed with everything that was suggested. She was so captivated by the way her music was expanding as well as the magical effect it had on her that he could have suggested they go to the moon, and she would have said yes. Nothing, he thought, could be more perfect.

The day he first touched her was a revelation. Not only because she didn't seem bothered by it, but it seemed to spur her on to new heights of expression in the music, as if she had been waiting for him to help her turn like a caterpillar into a butterfly. He fully intended to be the sunlight and warmth that encouraged the transformation.

His hand had fallen on her breast by accident when showing her a better way to hold the bow and instead of saying something, looking embarrassed or running away she had looked at him, her gaze challenging him to do even more, or so he thought.

When Hugh suggested closing the curtains in the music room 'to shield your eyes' he knew she understood it was so they couldn't be spied on. He was as certain of her complicity and agreement as he felt she was of his.

Over the weeks that followed, he tried out all types of sexual interactions and approaches, discovering the ones she enjoyed most.

He never forced her to do anything although he was careful to mention occasionally that this was a secret worth keeping.

He watched as she progressed from a gawky teenager into a confident siren. Her breasts responded to his loving touch becoming so magnificent he would bury his head in them. Hugh had no doubt she would be a beauty, her long copper hair and fair clear skin held wide-set blue eyes that had an intensity which moved him every time she looked at him.

Not once did she demure.

Not once did she say it was wrong.

At the end of the school year, he had dropped Alison. With no explanation her eyes constantly questioned his whenever their paths crossed.

Instead, he basked in the knowledge that Jenny loved him. She didn't have to say it, he could see it in the emotions that lingered there for him to pluck from the air around them.

Hugh would have given anything to know what was going on inside Jenny's head but instead, she always referred him to the music, saying that being touched helped her understand it even more.

Their practice sessions increased to three times weekly and became a dance of intimacy and longing interspersed with music and laughter. He loved her and held her for as long as he could for two hours, three times a week.

He spoke to her parents regularly who saw for themselves how fast her musical ability was developing. They were pleased and proud to have a daughter who was becoming well-known on the local social circuit and invited him into their home and lives little knowing what was going on beneath the surface.

CHAPTER SIX

Over the next few weeks, our paths crossed in a regular procession of practice sessions. As each one passed, I grew more confident until I unwittingly revealed the effect music had on me. It was the perfect C sharp that did it zoning into the perfect sweet spot. When our session finished, I noticed Mr Smithson watching me, smiling.

'You enjoy music don't you Jenny?'

'Yes.' I glanced away embarrassed.

When I looked back, he was standing. 'Would you like to join me for a coffee Jenny?'

I'd never been asked before and didn't hesitate with my agreement. I was confident my parents wouldn't mind, after all, they'd met him several times.

We sat in the town's local cafe, and I had my first cup of coffee. The coffee went straight to my head and I wondered if this was what it was like to be an adult.

We talked about music and Mr Smithson revealed he had hoped to become a professional pianist when he was younger but had lacked the skill. It explained a lot.

All too soon I was ushered out of the cafe and into his car.

'Tell me where you live, and I'll drop you off on my way home'.

I gave him directions and within a few minutes, he pulled in at the end of the driveway.

'I'll see you next week and perhaps we can have coffee again. You might want to mention it to your mother though, I wouldn't like her to worry.' He smiled encouragingly.

I felt comfortable and safe.

'You are late home Jenny?' My mother was putting the finishing touches to an arrangement of flowers in the kitchen with Mrs Jones when I pushed the door open with my foot.

'Mr Smithson invited me to the café in town because my practice went so well.'

'That's nice darling.' She barely heard what I'd said and when I mentioned he'd suggested we have coffee after future practices to talk about music she agreed on the proviso I was home before supper.

Mr Smithson accompanied me at the Christmas concert. He joined me for the New Year's Eve recital and at January's Burn's Night supper.

Slowly without realising, we became a 'couple', albeit an oddly matched one.

People got used to seeing us chatting in the cafe about music, often commenting on how rare it was to see such passion shared across the generations.

And somehow without me knowing just how it happened Miss Brough was replaced as my music teacher and our practice sessions increased from once to twice, and later three times a week.

It had also seemed perfectly natural that we increase lessons to two hours and my parents, having seen the improvements readily agreed. I think my father had set his sights on my becoming famous even then.

During one lesson Mr Smithson set up a tape recorder and recorded some of the pieces I was working on. We listened to the recording spotting and interpreting the errors I'd made and then trying refrains again and again until they were perfect.

I was so comfortable with him that it was okay for my body to do its own thing.

I never held back.

I didn't shy away from rapture.

And I never stopped the first time he touched me.

Each part of the practice, the music, his touch, my rapture, seemed an intrinsic part of the whole and I couldn't see how it could be separated.

When he suggested closing the curtains in the music room 'to shield your eyes against the light', it seemed perfectly reasonable because I was having difficulty concentrating on the score while hockey or lacrosse was going on in the playing fields beyond.

Lessons became as much about my exploration of physical boundaries as about music. The ability to dismiss the distraction I learnt at Mr Smithson's hands stood me in good stead when I later busked my way through college and University.

As my legs lengthened my mother complained I was growing out of clothes too quickly while Mr Smithson said he could see the beauty I would become.

I blossomed under his tutelage finding an inner confidence I'd never had before which extended to my performance and I was asked to play for so many local social events; weddings, funerals, and concerts, they all merged into one in my head.

Each practice ended in the same cafe with a coffee and a discussion about this week's piece. And every other comment contained a subtext for our extracurricular activities.

'Mr Smithson, do you think that if I move more in time with the music it will heighten my expression?'

'That's an interesting question Jenny and yes I do, perhaps we'll try it at your next lesson'.

And the next lesson could never come around quickly enough for me.

My parents were pleased the expensive instruments and lessons were so successful. But Diane and Victoria complained I was never available anymore for the things we had always done together.

'Are you coming to the cinema tonight?' Victoria would ask.

And I would shake my head and say no, I had another concert, another practice session or my parents were taking me out to celebrate some musical achievement or other.

'What is it with you and Mr Smithson anyway?' She would ask.

And I would just smile and say 'It's just music'.

The music discussion group had long since been abandoned by both Mr Smithson and Miss Brough.

She was jealous I think, but I can't be sure because I never asked her. I didn't want to go there in case she got too close and I revealed too much about what was really going on.

In later years, when we'd catch up for coffee after it had all ended she admitted she'd noticed but hadn't known what to say to wake me out of the dream. I couldn't criticise her and explained I probably wouldn't have listened to her anyway.

My parents, unlike my friends, never questioned the role that Mr Smithson played in my life inviting him to key occasions as an honorary member of the family.

They called him Hugh but to me, a child he was always Mr Smithson, even during our most intimate moments.

When the school year finished it came as no shock to anyone that I excelled in music in the end-of-year exams. And, as the lengthy summer holidays approached, I wondered how I would cope without his musical direction.

The problem was solved when Mr Smithson confirmed he had been asked to attend the annual summer music school as an accompanist.

It would be a whole two weeks of music at a country house some fifty miles from home. It was always a pleasure to be surrounded by students equally passionate about their music but this year that pleasure would have an added dimension.

I had requested and been granted my own room. It was part way up a tower with stunning views across open countryside. I never did find out where Mr Smithson was housed.

All students were required to attend lectures on a variety of subjects from the history of music to the music of mathematics and the physics of vibration.

My reactions to notes became clearer as I began to understand the scientific principles that lay behind my tuning fork body.

In one lecture we were asked to consider the concept of love in music. The discussion ranged from trying to pin down what love was to how it could be expressed by a musician.

I began to wonder in what context my experiences with Mr Smithson could be understood.

Already, I was confident it wasn't love.

CHAPTER SEVEN

'Mr Smithson'. Miss Dickson called him from across the playing field. 'Mr Smithson'.

He turned around to find her almost on top of him.

'Mr Smithson, the county summer school for music is coming up and they're looking for accompanists; I suggested you, I hope you don't mind'. She looked at him to gauge his reaction. 'I realise this is an imposition, but they were rather desperate as others have pulled out at short notice. Did you have anything planned for the summer?'

'As it happens I haven't made any plans yet, as you know my parents are no longer with me. What does it involve?' He asked the question already knowing the answer as Jenny had been full of excitement about it.

'You'll be needed for a fortnight, no longer and as we take a two-month summer break you should have plenty of time to add a holiday. They pay well and give bed and board, would that suit you?'

'Yes, that would suit very well indeed, who do I need to speak to about arrangements?'

'Oh, you don't have to worry about that, the arrangements will all come through me. I'll let you know as soon as I have the necessary details.' She turned on her heel and strode back to the school building, job done.

Three weeks later he was fifty miles away surrounded by dozens of children of varying ages carrying everything from recorders to double bass. He didn't see Jenny until she was almost on top of him.

'Hi.' she said. 'Have you settled in yet? My room is fabulous, overlooks the lake and everything and it's in that tower there. One of the perks of being older is I get my own room this year.' She looked at him archly, he understood exactly what she meant.

'That's great Jenny, you'll have to show me exactly where it is so I can collect you for practice sessions.' He spoke lightly knowing that other ears might be listening to their conversation.

'Why don't you come now, while we're all still muddling around? I don't have any practice until tomorrow and by then it may be too late to show you. When I've done that, I can go to my first lecture. It's exciting isn't it.' Her enthusiasm was infectious, and he laughed along with her.

Nights and days blended into one. Looking back years later Hugh wondered how he had stayed awake for the whole fortnight and supposed it was the heady mix of sex and secrecy.

Alison faded into distant memory. He realised his nights with her had been boring and desultory by comparison. This, he reflected, is what love is. The total and encompassing possession of another person within your own. Doing your bidding whilst they thought they were the piper.

He snatched sleep in his room during student lectures. His role was purely as accompanist which gave him plenty of free time alone with his thoughts. Aware of the irony Hugh reflected he was a harpist and she the harp, plucking her strings and making her dance in time to the beat of his heart, his head, his penis. He never wanted it to end.

But end it did. Fourteen days after it began it was all over and his torment began.

Jenny headed home collected by her parents to get ready for a long summer in France, and he headed back to his lonely flat.

Jenny had promised to write from France. But no letter or postcard arrived.

Moody and sullen, work colleagues meeting him in the street were snubbed and ignored. He was almost ready to drive to France and snatch her back from underneath the noses of her parents.

Then the letter arrived. Hand delivered, pushed through his letter box late at night he found it early the next morning and tore it open greedily.

Dear Hugh

I haven't seen you for weeks and I miss you. There's no easy way to say it, so I might as well come right out with it, I'm pregnant. I need to see you so we can talk about what we're going to do. Can you call, or write to me, as soon as possible, please?
Alison x

He re-read it several times before the contents finally sank in.

Pregnant, how could she be pregnant? It couldn't possibly be his as he had a note of her monthly dates in his diary. He never touched anyone, even Jenny, when she was likely to be fertile.

Thoughts rumbled through his head until he thought it might explode. The idea of going to France to bring Jenny back left his head immediately. This was all he needed, to be tied to a woman like Alison for the rest of his life.

Needing a coffee to clear his head he walked to the café he frequented with Jenny. The owner greeted him warmly. Hugh was one of his best customers and it always looked so well to have a mix of ages sat in the front window.

'Coffee please and make it strong. And plenty of sugar'. Hugh was aware he needed to keep his wits about him and needed the rush of caffeine to get him through the next few hours while he decided what to do.

He nursed the cup while his mind rolled around the problem. Marry Alison, that would be expected. He'd have to give up Jenny, but she was his best protégé yet and he couldn't, wouldn't do that. She couldn't be denied him because of a simple mistake.

Slowly, his mind turned to blame. This was Alison's fault, she should have been more careful and should have warned him she was highly fertile and likely to drop one at any time.

'Another coffee please … just like the first'.

'Problem's mate?' The owner brought over a fresh pot and poured it into the mug in front of Hugh.

'You could say that.' Hugh was terse and didn't look up.

'Anything I can help with?' Curiosity overcame his natural resistance to prying.

'Not unless you've got a magic wand and can wave away a woman for me.' Hugh finally looked at the owner. 'You don't happen to have such a thing, do you?'

The owner understood what wasn't being said immediately. 'Fraid not mate, but I do know someone you could speak to about things like this. You just wait here while I go and get a few details for you.'

He came back a few minutes later with a slip of paper in his hand. 'Here you go, you give this to your lady friend, she'll be sorted out in no time'.

Hugh took the paper and stuffed it in his pocket. 'Thanks, I owe you one.'

'No problem mate, it happens to us all at some time or another. Good luck.' The owner smiled encouragingly as he held the door open for Hugh to leave.

The response from Alison when he handed her the note of paper was not what he expected.

'How dare you suggest I get rid of the baby.'

The tears in her eyes almost moved him to relent but weren't quite enough to get him over what he would lose in return.

'I'm sorry Alison, but I can't marry you, I won't marry you and I don't want a child dragging me back all the time. I'm sorry but if you have this baby, you'll be doing it on your own, without me.'

He was, in his own mind, firm but fair. After all, she didn't have to go through with it. Women these days had choices, didn't they? It was up to her if she decided to keep the thing.

However, these things have a habit of creating intended consequences, and his was a summons to Miss Dickson's office one Tuesday afternoon.

'Mr Smithson, I understand that you are in some bother'. She didn't say what it was but knew enough to prevent him from lying.

'Yes, that's right Miss Dickson. I'm afraid Alison is pregnant.'

'Is it yours?'

It had never occurred to him that it wasn't his and he was tempted to say it might not be, but a small, insistent voice inside forced him to be honourable.

'Alison says it is and I believe her.' He was to the point saying no more than necessary.

'Are you planning to do the right thing?' She gave him no quarter, nowhere to go but out.

'I'm afraid not. I can't marry Alison even if I wanted to.'

'And why is that Mr Smithson?' Miss Dickson narrowed her eyes, she was a past master at spotting a lie in the making.

'Because I'm already married.' The lie tripped off his tongue easily and he tried out a small smile to emphasise the point.

'I see.' She turned her full gaze on him and stared him down, it was obvious to him she didn't believe him. 'You do realise this leaves me, the school, in a very difficult position, don't you?'

'I hadn't really thought about it if I'm honest.' And he hadn't, this was the first time it had started to cross his mind what the repercussions might be.

'I imagine that says a lot about the man you are then Mr Smithson.' Miss Dickson was like a judge handing down a sentence to the condemned man. 'I'm afraid I will be terminating your employment with immediate effect. Please collect your belongings from the staff room and your locker. The porter will take your staff badge and show you out.'

'But what about my teaching responsibilities, what about the pupils, you don't have a replacement?'

'You should have thought about that before being so cavalier with my staff Mr Smithson. I have already spoken to several possible replacements and am interviewing tomorrow. I'm sure we will find someone with a little more grace and dignity before the next school year begins. We will not, of course, provide you with a reference, so please do not expect one. Good day.' She turned in her chair and he was dismissed.

He collected his bits and pieces from the staff room and his locker as Mr Twigg waited for him to hand back his badge before locking him out of the building. He stalked back to his car incandescent with rage. How dare she dismiss him like he was a nobody. Deep inside though, he knew his anger stemmed from the reality of his situation. He would no longer have access to Jenny and without stealing her away, something he realised could never happen, it was over.

Several days later he left town and headed north leaving no forwarding address.

CHAPTER EIGHT

Summer school finished all too soon and the remainder of the long school holiday was spent en famille in France. The only connection with Mr Smithson was violin practice and the occasional postcard written but never sent. I noticed not minding the enforced separation after all, it wasn't as if I loved the man. I had already realised that ours was never going to be a happy-ever-after story.

My parents were indulgent. I'd far exceeded their expectations in all my exams and my report from summer school had said I was 'exceptionally talented with a rare gift for musical expression'. For my part, I was happy enough to play the role of the perfect daughter; speaking when spoken to, taking part in conversations with their adult friends and murmuring appreciative comments about the art we saw, the places we visited and the food we ate.

More than once they commented on my maturity, my confidence and my ability to hold my own in adult company, frequently and loudly comparing me favourably with the children of other friends who committed the sin of acting like the teenagers they were. Little did they realise that my misdemeanours would have far outweighed those of my contemporaries had they been put on a balance scale.

This was the France we knew well and our villa is still a favourite bolt-hole today. We were already well known amongst the other British families and villagers who lived in the area as my parents had always been careful to arrange several sets of suitable 'play' dates since I was young and we'd first bought the villa.

There was one family we always seemed to spend a lot of time with; Miriam and Jeremy with James, David, and Sally; known to family and friends as Jamie, Davey and Sal.

It soon became clear that the dynamics of our friendships had changed since the previous summer. Jamie, now 17, was itching to get on with life. Davey at 14 was testing out the sullen look and Sal, who was almost 12, had found a new set of friends much more suited to her latent interest in make-up and boys.

After lunch, both sets of parents would sit in the garden while we children dipped in and out of the pool or played games when we could muster up the energy.

The sultry afternoons passed in a hazy blur, merging one into another. It was hot, stifling really and none of us felt much like being energetic. I always claimed one of the pool loungers as my own, hauling it to a convenient spot for climbing in and out of the cool water. I kept everything I needed close by; sunglasses, a hat, a jug of lemonade, the current book and a towel I could stretch out on to brown whilst listening to my mother reminding me about suntan lotion every hour or so.

Suddenly, I was aware of a shadow between the sun and me. I remember opening one eye to find Jamie staring at my body.

He claimed he didn't mean to wake me up. I wasn't convinced. It seemed that was exactly what he intended but I had neither strength nor heart to argue about it.

'It's OK, I wasn't asleep anyway, just toasting to a nice shade of crisp.' I smiled to show it didn't matter.

He sat down on the edge of the lounger. 'Can I sit down?'

'Looks like you already have.' I said it without rancour and smiled at him, it was good to change the activity of the afternoon anyway as the heat had begun to dissipate and I had a little more energy.

He looked embarrassed and glanced away.

'It's OK, honestly. Did you want anything in particular?' I was genuinely interested in his errand. After all, it was the first time he'd done something other than pour cold water over me in a game of tag. I think my curiosity was piqued and I wondered if had he matured as I had over the last year.

He looked at me. Really looked at me, perhaps for the first time ever. Then shading his eyes he checked where the parents were; all four were still deep in conversation over the second, or was it the third bottle of the afternoon?

'You look different this year.' He began diffidently. It was obvious he was working up to something but hadn't quite found the right words.

'I'm a year older than last year and Mum keeps complaining I'm still growing out of clothes too quickly.' I tried to help him out, but from his sullen expression, it was clear this wasn't what he meant. To be honest I knew where he was going already, my sixth sense and patience had been honed through pitch-perfect tuition with Mr Smithson. I could wait it out until he found his way.

'That's not really what I meant …. I don't know how to put it …. You look like an adult …. a proper one, not a teenager playing at being one.' His words came staggering out as if he wasn't sure how I'd react. Between each statement, he watched my face and I'm pretty sure my lack of expression was no help whatsoever.

Putting my hat on to shade my eyes, I took my sunglasses off and focused on his face.

'What do you mean?' I was genuinely interested in where he was going. Was it something other people had noticed but been too polite, or shy to say? And perhaps the biggest question of all, why hadn't my parents said anything?

'You look like a model in one of those bra adverts. You know the ones with the big eyes, big tits whose look is just daring you to take it off, but you know you'll never have the nerve.'

I was flattered. I hadn't thought about what I looked like and assumed I was just like all the other girls, gangly, awkward and spotty. Perhaps Mr Smithson was right when he claimed my breasts were 'magnificent'.

Moving slightly, I arched my back a little to give them a little more prominence, dropped my chin, opened my eyes wide and stared at James 'Like this?'

He got up from the lounger quickly and turned round so I couldn't see his face. 'Yes, just like that.'

I got up too pulled my sundress over my head and slipped my sandals on. I grabbed my tote bag stuffing my sunbathing accoutrements in haphazardly.

'Mum, we're going for a walk.' I shouted over to the four adults who were deep in conversation.

She waved her hand at me. 'Don't be back late darling.'

I nodded in acquiescence and smiled.

Grabbing Jamie's hand, I pulled him around the pool and into the woods with me. He had the sense not to argue and just followed. Once we were out of sight I dropped his hand and slowed the pace to a stroll, it might be getting cooler but that was relative, it was still too hot to be energetic.

'Remind me, how old are you now?' I asked.

'I'll be 18 in October. I'm off to uni next year. Just got the A levels to pass and then I'm gone.' Jamie smiled as he spoke. It was clear he was looking forward to the freedom that university afforded and I was right when I recognised the need to be off out into the world.

'You're a couple of years ahead of me. I'll be 16 in February and am going to music college next September.' Saying that gave me a shiver, as I thought about the next stage of my life and where I seemed to be headed.

'So, when did you grow up then? You were still a little kid last summer and now you seem older than me.' It was the first honest thing he'd said in the whole encounter so far.

I thought back to the previous summer and realised it was true. I was definitely not on his 'hit list' back then. Thinking about it there had been a lot of sighing and pointed comments about 'kiddies playing' directed at his siblings and me.

In reply, I asked a question of my own. 'Have you ever had sex, Jamie?'

He obviously wasn't expecting such a question and his eyes bulged and cheeks turned a satisfying shade of beetroot. 'Yes … of course ….' His answer didn't hold water. I'd already had enough experience to know when someone was lying about this particular topic.

'Are you sure James?' I glanced at him. Perhaps it was my use of his full name that got his attention rather than the challenge in the question.

He had the grace to look sheepish. Perhaps it was my voice or the way I asked the question that caused him to think again and reflect on his answer.

'Well …..' his unspoken words hung in the air; not yet, not for lack of effort, etc. I could hear them all echoing.

'Have you?' James was covering his embarrassment by hoping I'd have some too.

My look was cool and direct. 'Yes.' Just a simple answer but the teenager in me was still strong enough to want to score points and I knew this one would be a direct hit.

We walked for a while without speaking. Jamie, I knew, had a lot to mull over and I was wondering why I'd broken my promise not to tell. There was obviously more going on inside my head than I'd previously thought. It occurred to me I wanted to show off, to be better than him and, if I looked closely enough, to make him jealous.

The last thought was the most disturbing. I'd known Jamie for as long as I could remember. Our families had spent the long lazy weeks of summer and some Christmas holidays together since we'd been toddlers. I'd never thought of him as anything other than a friend. Did this mean I'd changed, he'd changed or we'd both changed? We never met or conversed anywhere other than in France and sometimes a whole year would go by with only a mutual Christmas card to show for the bond that existed between the two families.

We trod a familiar path heading towards open farmland on the edge of the wood. We both knew that if we carried on through the field, we'd hit the dunes that bordered our little part of the Baie d'Audierne. We'd made the trek frequently enough with towels, beach balls and picnics to do it in our sleep if needed.

This time though, instead of heading down the well-worn route we both knew, I headed off to the right around the back of a wheat field alongside the wood. I didn't want to be where other people were if I was going to explore this new thought a little more. Jamie followed two steps behind and suddenly it seemed to me he was the lackey and I the leader; it was up to me to show the right way practically and metaphorically.

Unlike some fields in France, this one was not too large and still bordered by hedges thick with wild fruit bushes and trees. The autumn would bring a good harvest. Once again, I mourned the fact we wouldn't be there in September when the blackberries were ripe and juicy. I sighed, I'd need to satisfy that craving at home.

We wandered into the next field, this was a direction the families had never taken as it led away from both house, village, and beach. It did, however, lead to my particular bit of solitude, the one I escaped to when the pressures of coping with a large group overcame the need to change my status as an only child.

'Where are we going?' Jamie's voice carried along behind me 'I don't think I've ever been down this way before.'

'Just a bit further and you'll see.' I glanced back over my shoulder and smiled encouragingly.

Without warning the field and woodland gave way to a pale purple mass of lavender. You couldn't really call it a field, it wasn't big enough. The air was heavy with scent and insects. Whenever I walked this part of the path, I felt a little like Dorothy and was tempted to lie down and sleep. Fortunately, this time I had the human equivalent of Toto with me!

'Wow, I didn't know this was here, Mum would love it. She's always after lavender for stuff at the village hall.' Jamie's voice was strident, breaking into my thoughts.

Why had I brought him this way, I didn't want anyone else finding my idyll and spoiling it. So far no one I knew had discovered my secret and here I was handing it to Miriam on a plate. I could have kicked myself. I carried on walking, not trusting myself to speak.

Jamie must have sensed my displeasure, 'Did I say something wrong?'

'Look, it's not my business who knows about this place.' I tried to keep my voice steady 'It's just I've never shared it with anyone else before and I rather like it being just me … and now you.' I added the last as an afterthought.

Jamie caught up with me and touched my arm to get my attention, 'Sorry. I didn't realise it was private.'

He watched me closely, gauging my reaction and I relented. 'Don't worry about it, perhaps we'll keep it our secret?' The question hung between us and Jamie's quick nod showed he understood.

I turned away and onto a barely visible path that cut a diagonal through the lavender. When we came to the far side of the field it became apparent that what looked like a flat plain down towards the dunes hid a shallow depression pressed into the earth. Surrounded by trees whose tops skimmed the surface of the surrounding land like bushes it provided a cool and shady place to sit and think a day away.

I had always thought of it as my Fairy Dell after discovering it when my parents deemed me old enough to roam outside the confines of the villa alone. In the middle was a hollow tree that was perfect for storing cold drinks and sandwiches, It also housed an old blanket and a cushion. I shook them out to encourage the spiders and bugs to drop off and then spread them out below the tree on a handy pile of leaves.

'I come here to think.' I explained to Jamie who sat down beside me. 'It's quiet, warm and nice to feel the air on your body.' I looked at him, I wasn't sure he would understand my oblique comment.

Sure enough, it took a few seconds before it registered. 'Oh, naked you mean?'

'Naked as the day.' I agreed.

'What if someone comes?' His concern was genuine; for himself though, probably not for me.

'No one ever has, at least not while I've been coming and anyway, we've all seen a naked body before even if it's just our own, it's not that unusual you know.' I smiled

Standing up I hauled off my sundress, untied my bikini top and slipped off the knickers and lay on my back on the blanket closing my eyes, enjoying gentle puffs of air as they played across my belly.

I was aware of Jamie standing up and then lying down again. Opening one eye I could see he too had decided to join me. I reached out to find his hand and grasped it, he returned the grasp and we lay still.

Behind my sunglasses I watched the sun play on the leaf canopy overhead and the stately way it moved across the sky, casting a shadow here and a sunburst there. I was acutely aware of Jamie by my side but didn't feel a need to do anything other than lie next to him. I had no idea how he might be feeling, but assumed he felt the same; after all, he hadn't moved towards me once.

The silence between us was deafening but the sounds of nature made up for our lack. As soon as we stilled the wood came back to life. Wood Pigeons cooed, scuttling creatures searched the undergrowth in search of a tasty morsel, and in the distance a cat mewed. The bees and insects were busy doing their job, buzzing about with great intensity, but never once landing on me.

I must have fallen asleep as suddenly the sun was no longer high in the sky and the air had noticeably cooled without me realising. I shivered and sat up, letting go of Jamie's hand. He mumbled something and turned over, clearly sleep had yet to release its grip on him. Pulling my clothes back on I took the chance to look at him more carefully, comparing his body to Mr Smithson.

Muscles were beginning to form underneath his arms and across his back and chest. He was going to be well-built. Sandy hair flopped over his eyes; his mouth slightly parted sat in a face which already contained the haughty look hinting towards becoming handsome. Breeding shows I thought, realising Mr Smithson had none of the features I normally associated with one of my class.

At some deep level, Jamie must have been aware I was staring. 'Are you going to spend all day here?'

'I'm cold.' I shivered for added effect 'I think I must have fallen asleep and the sun's gone over.'

'Time to go then.' Jamie hauled himself upright and pulled on his shorts and tee shirt.

I hadn't realised he had no underpants on earlier and watched his penis as it disappeared behind the shorts.

Jamie caught me looking, 'How do I compare?' he asked the question lightly despite his obvious schoolboy concern.

Smiling, I caught his hand and winked. 'Very well Jamie …. very well indeed.'

'Can we do this again?'

'Yes, if you'd like.' I was being coy, I knew.

'I'd like that a lot … and … maybe next time I'll kiss you.'

'Yes Jamie, and maybe I'll let you.' My response was playful even as I realised, I was looking forward to that event as much as he was, if his grin was anything to go by.

Grabbing his hand again, I led him out of the dell and we reversed the path we'd trodden earlier.

'There you are, I was beginning to get worried about you.' My mother's greeting was underpinned by the large outdoor table with five others sitting around it helping themselves to salads and quiche.

'You must have taken a long walk … did you get as far as the beach?' Jeremy's question had a hint of threat about it. Unspoken words hung in the air ready to fall on our heads as soon as we let slip what we'd been up to.

'Almost, but not quite. Did you know there's some spectacular scenery around here Mum, it would be perfect for painting, especially if you head off round the back of the wood that way.' As he spoke he pointed left and I was grateful. Jamie's response, smooth and disarming, had the desired effect and the conversation turned away from our adventures towards trips out with paper and pastels.

By the time the evening closed, the families had bonded ever more tightly and there were promises of spending the following day together again, this time at their villa.

'Tomorrow?' I handed the question to Jamie quietly as they were leaving. He nodded before running to catch up with Davey and Sal.

Jamie and I became 'an item' on that holiday.

Our parents and Jamie's siblings all seemed pleased by the joining of two families, and we were positively encouraged to go off for long, 'romantic' walks to cement 'young love', as my mother kept putting it.

Looking back, I think she was pleased I'd finally shown an interest in something other than my violin, that I was a normal teenage girl and wasn't going to turn out 'odd'.

To the outside world, we were walking, hand in hand, around the French countryside. Sometimes we'd take bikes and a picnic and head off to the lonelier stretches of the beach, laying out towels for sunbathing and skinny dipping. But mostly, we ended up at the dell, it was a quiet refuge from the comments and the observation of immediate family and the wider expat community of which we were a part.

Jamie was quickly comfortable being naked in my company and was usually quicker at stripping off before laying back to watch me take my clothes off slowly, deliberately, provocatively, stretching up my arms in what I hoped was a passable facsimile of Paul Philippe's Awakening.

That first summer we never progressed further than kissing. I think unconsciously I knew it would spoil our burgeoning relationship if we took it any further. And Jamie seemed content to just enjoy being in my company. We talked about sex of course, but by mutual consent agreed it would be something we might do later. When 'later' might be we never discussed, we just knew that now was not the right time.

It never occurred to me that what I was doing might be construed by some as being unfaithful to Mr Smithson. After all, he was my music teacher, not someone I ever thought I'd spend any other time with. I appreciated what he'd done for me, both for my music and my sexuality, but that was as far as it went. And it never crossed my mind that in his loneliness he might be bothered by my lack of regard.

CHAPTER NINE

Over the next few weeks' Summer receded towards Autumn, nights felt cooler, and the days lost a little of their brightness. We began packing up the villa in preparation for leaving. Miriam and Jeremy did the same and at the end of August we all left, Jamie to his bit of the Dorset countryside and me to the wild Norfolk coast.

Just before returning to school, I heard that Mr Smithson wouldn't be there. It seemed he'd moved north unexpectedly in response to a family crisis of some description. I was disappointed but realised that I wasn't sad, I accepted that the previous year had been an anomaly and was soon taken up with my music and other subjects.

Jamie and I wrote to each other weekly, talking about the dramas of school, the antics of our friends and the vagaries of our parents. Victoria and Diane featured heavily in mine as our friendship reignited now that Mr Smithson was no longer around to divert my attention.

My parents had changed too and appeared to have done an about-turn since we'd come back from France. Whilst they had been quite happy to let me do my own thing the previous year they now became clingy wanting to know where I was, who I was with and why I hadn't been back by curfew. I assumed it was because I was leaving home at the end of the school year and indulged them, answering their constant questions about where I was going, who I was with and what we were doing with as much grace as possible.

My tactic must have worked as they slowly dropped their nosiness to a manageable level when they saw I was working hard, getting good results and my music hadn't suffered following the unexpected departure of Mr Smithson.

The year turned, and at Christmas both families were once again in France, sharing cosy evenings in front of log-burning stoves and crisp walks to 'blow the cobwebs away'.

Jamie and I found as many opportunities to get away on our own as possible, this time though we spent our time fully clothed, it was far too cold to be naked even if it was in our favourite spot. We walked to the local bar and drank coffee with our French and ex-pat friends. On Christmas day, when the parents were too far gone to notice, and Davey and Sal were at a party, we sneaked upstairs and spent a quiet couple of hours kissing on his bed as we both felt the time was still not right to take it any further.

Jamie never asked who I'd had sex with, and he never asked me to compare them to him again. Part of me wanted to tell him, but an even bigger part felt the time would never be right to share what had made me into the woman I was becoming. I instinctively felt he would never understand, and it would be a hurdle we might never get over.

We all headed home again at the beginning of January after one last New Year's Eve party. This time it was harder to leave Jamie, and my parents indulged my tears as far as Calais before finally ordering me to stop. Our letters became more frequent and more personal. I started telling him how I felt, and he reciprocated telling me he missed me. We didn't use the L word; it, like sex, seemed to belong to our future, not the present we were creating.

My 16th birthday coincided with a weekend that year and as a treat, my parents took me to London to see a show. I forget which one now because they neglected to tell me they had invited Jamie to join us for the day too.

They sent us off on our own and we whiled away a few hours at the Natural History Museum, dipping into the tearoom a couple of times to sit and talk about what we'd seen. The necklace he gave me was beautiful, amethyst set in silver on a long silver chain. I promised never to take it off.

'You're beautiful, you know.' He spoke quietly as he fastened the necklace around my neck.

I blushed and mindful that I'd been taught to accept compliments gracefully, said thank you. I could feel his grey eyes looking at me seriously and stared back.

'You are you know, I wanted to tell you at Christmas, but I think I love you …. yes, I think I love you.' He faltered in his speech as he said the words we had both held back from saying for so many months.

I was only 16 and still too young to appreciate how significant it was and laughed it off.

'You don't know me, Jamie. You only know what you've seen and what I've written. You don't know the other me, the one that came before.' I spoke the words lightly, hoping to convey as much meaning as I could through what I didn't say as much as what I did.

Jamie grabbed my hand across the table saying, 'I know enough to know I want to know you better and for longer.'

'Do you really, do you want to know me better?' I wanted the answer to be yes, I wanted to be swept away by the torrents of emotion I already knew could exist between a man and a woman.

I'd experienced enough with Mr Smithson to know I had a great capacity for passion that had yet to be filled. Instinctively I knew this had also maimed me, skewing the idea of passionate love into one frequented by power and control.

In answer, Jamie pulled me out of the seat and pulled me to the Jurassic exhibits.

'This is where I belong, I live on the Jurassic coast and it's been around a very long time, millions of years. And this is how long I will love you for.' He swept his arm around the gallery to emphasise the point and I capitulated, I fell into his arms safe in the knowledge I would always have Jamie.

The remainder of the weekend passed in a happy blur, a meal, a show, a goodbye at Waterloo station with Jamie and then a hotel for my parents and me. When I eventually got to bed, it was to dream of Jamie and his coast, I settled down in the certain knowledge I would be loved for life.

CHAPTER TEN

At Easter, my parents were too busy to travel to France and they agreed, with a lot of cajoling from me and agreement from Miriam and Jeremy, that I could travel alone to stay with Jamie and his family.

The journey was long. A car trip to Norwich, the 'fast', apparently, train to London, the boat train from St Pancras to Dover and finally the ferry to Calais where Miriam and Jeremy would collect me.

It was while crossing London I spotted Mr Smithson on the opposite platform as we passed through Farringdon. The shock I felt was unexpected; he appeared to have aged. He had a beard and was wearing a shirt and tie. His louche look had been replaced by a degree of respectability. I couldn't help staring and he must have felt my eyes on him as he looked straight at me sitting in the train as it pulled into the station.

Grabbing my bags, I leapt from the train just before the doors closed. The train pulled out and I saw he had started towards the exit.

'Stop', I shouted across the station, 'Mr Smithson'.

He stopped and looked at me, then shook his head and carried on. Dodging the waiting crowds, I ran for the stairs, taking them two at a time not noticing the weight of my bags in my hands. I crisscrossed the tunnels until I found the one leading down to the other platform, but it was empty. He was gone.

Perhaps I'd been mistaken, perhaps it wasn't him after all, perhaps he'd shaken his head when I called his name because it wasn't him. All the possible reasons for his disappearance from the platform flooded my head and my senses. I couldn't comprehend that after all we'd shared just a few months earlier, he might not want to see me. I needed a consolation, and my only recourse was to assume I'd been mistaken.

Eventually, I arrived at St Pancras and caught my train with minutes to spare. The remainder of the journey was uneventful although I found myself going over the incident again and again, trying to see it from a different angle or perspective that would explain why I had mistaken someone else for Mr Smithson.

The channel crossing was calm, and the engines lulled me into a light doze. A light bump informed my semi-conscious brain we had arrived, and I opened my eyes to bright sunshine; it was a glorious day. I made my way to the outer deck straining my eyes to see my surrogate family, especially Jamie and I spotted them waving madly from the car park and waved back, promptly forgetting the encounter at Farringdon.

It was good to be back in the familiar routine. Still too cold for naked, it was warm enough to be out on the beach in a jumper and jeans and this time we invited Sal and Davey along too. All four of us played tag with the surf, daring each other to get wet.

It was the first time we'd ever slept in the same house together and, even if no one else could feel it, the tension for us was palpable. The letters Jamie and I had written were in the back of both our minds and we were shy in our own company. Holding hands was as close as we came to any form of sexual contact for the whole break. But it was enough; our friendship was morphing into something deeper, and I had a sense we were both content with the transition

By the end of the Easter holidays, Miriam and Jeremy were confident enough that Jamie and I were not getting up to anything untoward to invite me to stay for a couple of weeks at the end of June. By then Jamie would have finished his A levels and I would have finished most of my 'O' levels. My parents accepted enthusiastically on my behalf and then promptly booked themselves a holiday in the Maldives as compensation. I didn't mind, I was looking forward to seeing Jamie's home and meeting his friends.

Our letters became more ardent. Jamie began to tell me the things he'd like to do with me, and it wasn't going to the pictures or walking on the beach. I started to tell him the things I liked, and they weren't books or music. We built a picture of each other that existed outside of our reality to date. Now that I was 16 and had reached the legal age of consent, we both skirted around the topic of sex, both of us hoping it would be soon, but at the same time wanting it to remain in the future so we could enjoy the anticipation longer.

I no longer thought about Mr Smithson. I'd all but forgotten him and the strange incident in London had receded from my memory. Instead, it was Jamie I imagined doing the things I had once enjoyed in the school music room. I wondered just how much I would be able to tell him about what I liked and how music made my body and heart sing.

My music had flourished despite the disappearance of my tutor, and it became apparent to everyone who heard me that I would indeed fulfil my father's wish and become a professional musician. My parents had already decided I would board at St Cecilia's College when it came time to do A levels and, after auditioning, took me on a trip around Manchester. The highlight was a lunchtime concert at the Halle by current students from St Cecilia's.

As we settled into our seats I glanced around, checking out the rest of the audience. My eyes came to rest on the profile of Mr Smithson sitting several rows ahead of us to the right. I don't think he'd seen us as his gaze was fixed on the stage.

I watched him covertly from behind my programme unable to decide if his look was positive or not. It seemed feline, the same look my aunt's cat had when it was stalking a mouse or bird in the garden. Looking at the stage I tried to make out what he was staring at.

The ensemble was seated and ready to begin. The conductor raised his baton, and the first violin lifted her instrument ready to begin. I held my breath. This was the moment the music came to life, and I was looking forward to seeing how someone else nuanced the piece we were listening to.

My mother noticed it first. The way she raised her head to look you straight in the eye, how her back arched in time to the rise and fall of the tempo.

'That girl, the viola, she looks just like you do when you play darling.' She whispered before turning her attention back to the stage.

I looked again seeing for the first time the gestures and movements that marked out someone who felt the music as much as heard it. I glanced back at Mr Smithson and sure enough it was her he was watching.

I wondered if she was his student too and if she'd had the same 'education' I'd had. There was no rancour in my thought, just a tacit acknowledgement that I probably wasn't the first and certainly wouldn't be the last. I thought about mentioning his presence to my parents after all, they had been as shocked as me to find he had left so unexpectedly the previous year. I thought better of it, some inner warning suggested I might not like the consequences of doing so, but I resolved to try and 'bump' into him during the interval.

'Stop drumming your fingers darling, it's very distracting.' My mother hissed.

I hadn't been aware of doing so and as soon as she mentioned it, I noticed my feet were tapping too; not with the beat, just with impatience for the first half of the performance to end.

As soon as the ensemble had stood to take a bow, I made my excuses about needing the bathroom and fled through the nearest exit. I intended to make my way to the back of the auditorium and meet Mr Smithson at the door nearest him. Glancing back, I saw he was just making his way along his row towards the aisle and picked up the pace.

I tripped over him at the door and we both took a tumble.

'I'm so sorry, I didn't see you.' I was overcome with embarrassment, this wasn't the way I'd hoped to meet him again. I'd have preferred to be adult and cool, instead I felt childish, red and sweaty.

'It's no problem, please don't worry ...' The sentence trailed off when he realised who he'd collided with. 'Jenny ... I didn't expect to see you here ... are you alone?' He was nervous and began looking along the corridor to see if he could spot someone he knew.

'I'm with my parents, they're over there at the front and I'm sure they would love to catch up with you if you have a moment.' As soon as I said it, I knew it would never happen.

'I couldn't possibly intrude.' he said. 'I'm just leaving as it happens, I can't stay.'

I knew he was lying, he realised I knew it too.

'Listen Jenny don't tell your parents you've seen me, I'm sure they wouldn't be happy to know we met up.'

I was curious now. 'Why did you leave last year?' I put on my guileless face, the one I used to great effect to get what I wanted with Mum and

Dad. I knew there was more to his leaving than had been said and his comment had confirmed it; I wanted to know what it was.

'I didn't choose to leave. I had to leave. I have elderly parents and they needed looking after Jenny. It just seemed like the right time to make that decision.'

There was something about his face, something in the way he formed the sentence that didn't sound right, and I wanted to know more, to understand. But as luck would have it for him, the bell rang for the end of the interval summoning us back to our seats.

I looked at him again. 'You didn't even say goodbye.' And with that turned on my heel and headed back to my parents and safety.

'Where were you Jenny, we looked but couldn't find you, you missed your drink?' My mother was accusatory.

I appeased her with a look that said I didn't feel well and rubbed my belly. She understood immediately, pushing the hair back from my face and holding my hand.

'You can have some water and an aspirin when we get back to the hotel.' She smiled and turned back to the stage to watch the remainder of the performance.

I glanced back to where Mr Smithson had been sitting, he was gone!

CHAPTER ELEVEN

The June break loomed large on the horizon and the countdown to my trip to Dorset and Jamie's family home began. I had passed the audition for St Cecilia's with flying colours and would even receive a scholarship much to the delight of my father.

My 'O' level exams started in earnest, and I spent increasing amounts of time in my room revising and practising. The regime at St Cecilia's would be punishing, with 10 to 15 hours of formal practice every week, more if I wanted to excel. By the time I emerged at the end of term, I was spent. Exhausted and white-faced I couldn't face another book, essay, or even pick up a pen. Even my violin was put aside for the fortnight. I would have one more exam when I got back but that was it, my time at Jamieson's was over.

Victoria, Diane and I cried buckets on our last day at school. It felt like everything was ending, although, in reality, it was just beginning for each of us. They were staying on in the sixth form together, I promised to write from Manchester and tell them all about college life.

'You're so lucky you know, my parents would never let me go off to another part of the country just to do my 'A' levels.' Victoria moaned.

'I'm not going for 'A' levels you know that, they're just something else I have to do on top of the music, you know that. And besides, you'd never do the work.' I smiled at her.

She smiled back. 'You're right, I'm not that interested in school to bother. As long as I get the grades I need for Uni then that's enough for me, I don't want to be some hoity-toity famous musician like you do.'

Diane laughed. 'Listen to the pair of you, you'll be home for the holiday Jenny and we'll see you then, and you can phone and write and you never know we might all end up at the same Uni afterwards too.'

I held their hands for as long as I could before my mother called me back to the car so we could leave.

I waved and waved until they were dots on the horizon as we drove away and into the future.

My parents and I all caught the same train to London, they were heading to Heathrow to catch their flight whilst I was once again battling across London this time to catch a train from Waterloo to Dorchester. I wondered if I'd see Mr Smithson again but wasn't surprised when I didn't after all, I was on a completely different line.

Jamie was waiting at the station to meet me. Without telling me, he'd passed his driving test and was now the proud owner of a Mini Cooper, an 18th birthday present from his parents.

Holding me tight, he smelt my hair and nuzzled into my neck. 'It's good to see you.'

I pushed him back so I could see him properly and smiled. 'You look tired, been stopping out late?'

'It's the 'A' levels, if I'd realised they would be as difficult as they were I wouldn't have done them. I'm glad they're out of the way though and I've now got a whole four months with nothing to do but drive the lanes picking up stray girls from stations and ravishing them.'

I laughed and punched him in the arm. 'There had better not be any other stray girls making out in your car, that's my prerogative.'

His home was beautiful. Mellow and warm in the sunlight with a terrace running the length of its back and around one side. It was as picture-perfect as all the photographs he'd sent, and I was looking forward to roaming the grounds with him. I was sure there must be a hidden dell somewhere.

As his car drew up in the driveway Sal ran out to meet us. She hugged me hard, grabbed my hand and pulled me through the open French windows. Miriam and Jeremy were reading and looked up with amusement at my grand entrance.

'Be careful Sal, she's only just arrived and won't take kindly to having her arm removed from its socket just yet.' Jeremy got up and gave me a quick hug.

Miriam came over too. 'It's so nice to see you Jenny, Jamie has been moping about for the last week waiting for your exams to finish and Sal, as you can see, has made lots of plans for things you girls can do together.'

She smiled at her daughter indulgently while my heart sank. I'd hoped this might be the holiday that Jamie and I finally made it past the kissing stage. I was pretty sure he was hoping for the same thing too.

Smiling weakly, I put on my best-behaved guest face. 'Can I use the loo please I need to pee?'

'Sal will show you where to go and she'll show you to your room too. Don't worry about the bags I'll ask Peter to bring them up for you after he's brought in tea, you look like you could do with something hot.'

'It's going to be such fun'. Sal grabbed my hand to take me through the door into the hallway. 'There's so much to do around here and there are so many things I want to show you.'

I couldn't help being charmed by her enthusiasm and squeezed her hand back. Glancing back, I spotted Jamie coming into the drawing room, he smiled and waved as I disappeared dragged by Sal up the stairs.

My room was pretty and quiet. A bed, chest of drawers, wardrobe and small sink were all I needed for the week. It was next door to Sal's room, and I wondered briefly just how much noise might filter through the old building's walls. I fully intended to make use of both this room and Jamie's if I could help it.

I washed off the grime of the journey as well as I could and peed in our shared bathroom. Looking at myself in the mirror it was clear, even to me, that I needed some sun. My pasty face was blotchy, and I had the beginnings of spots on my chin and forehead. I wrinkled my nose in disgust hoping that Jamie would still like me enough to carry through on the promise of our letters.

Making my way back downstairs I could hear the whole family in the drawing room long before I saw them. Davey had arrived too, looking older than when I'd seen him at Easter. At 15 he was putting on height and weight and would soon be the same size as his older brother. He smiled and said hello, drawing me into a welcome hug.

'Here you go, tea, that's what you need; and some of Mrs Laxton's wonderful Victoria sponge.' Miriam passed me a plate and a teacup. Setting it on the table next to me I looked at the family as if for the first time.

I'd often wondered what it might be like to be more than one and now I had a feeling it would have been nice to have had brothers or sisters I could spend time with, rather than it always being my parents or school friends.

'You look like you need some sun and the fresh air.' Miriam was always to the point with her comments.

'I could take you into the gardens and show you the swing and climbing trees.' Sal offered.

I was very grateful when her mother intervened. 'I suspect Jamie might want to show her around Sal. Don't worry you'll get some time together too, just not today.'

Jamie smiled. 'Don't worry Sal we'll all go down to the beach tomorrow with a picnic so we can swim and sunbathe.'

Sal was mollified and returned to her book.

That afternoon Jamie took me uphill and down dale. The estate was extensive, much larger than my own home in Norfolk. He showed me the rhododendrons that were still blooming, the stream they had fished in as children and the estate church all his ancestors had married and been buried in.

'You look even more tired than I was after my exams. Are you OK?' He was kind and solicitous.

'I'm fine, I just need a break from everything for a few days, you know get away from books and things. A bit of fresh air and the beach sounds like fun.' I smiled at him and held out my hand. 'Come on, I'll race you back to the house.' And took off at a pace.

Jamie, being longer-legged and fresh, won with seconds to spare.

'That wasn't fair, you haven't just had a seven-hour journey.' I tried to look petulant, but the run had done me good, it got my blood flowing, and I was feeling brighter.

He laughed. 'Come on, there's just one more place I want to show you, you'll love it.' Jamie grabbed my hand and dragged me to the front of the house, along the drive and then ducked into the shrubs on his right.

We pushed our way through, following a little rabbit path, it seemed dense and never-ending until, suddenly we were out the other side and in a small clearing surrounded by high trees and dense undergrowth.

'This is my place.' he said. 'This is where I come when I need to get away from the others and it reminds me of our valley in France. I come here now to think about you.' He paused. 'This will be our place from now on, we can come here just to be quiet, alone if you like. Davey and Sal don't know about it, they never wanted to go through the thicket, so it's private, very private.'

His meaning was clear. 'This is wonderful Jamie do you want to stay awhile?'

He nodded saying 'I'd love to, but we've already been out too long, and the parents will be wondering where we've got to I'm sure.'

As we slowly made our way back through the shrubbery I kept the thought of what might happen over the next two weeks close to my heart.

The following morning, I woke to the sounds of a flute worming its way through the open window. I stuck my head out and realised it was coming from Sal's room.

Pulling on my dressing gown I went next door, knocking gently to let her know I was there.

She carried on playing, I recognised Telemann's Suite in A minor and settled on her bed to hear her out.

She paused for breath and put her flute down.

'I didn't know you were a musician too Sal, you never said.' I looked at her.

She looked away. 'I didn't want to tell you, you are so good I was afraid you would think I was silly. I told the others not to tell you too. They all thought I was mad.'

I was enthusiastic in my response. 'You're very good you know, that's grade three and was almost performance-perfect.'

'It's one of my favourites and I play it to warm up, it's less boring than scales.' She smiled.

I smiled back. 'I know what you mean Sal, sometimes I go to my favourite pieces instead of scales, but I always get my knuckles rapped if I do it too much as it shows when I practice.' I paused. 'You should have said, I'd have brought my violin with me, and we could have practised together.'

'That would be nice.' She was shy. 'I'd like to play with you too.'

'Perhaps I can accompany you instead. I'm not very good, the piano is my second instrument, and I don't practice as much as I should, but if you can ignore the missed notes and stumbles I'll give it a go.'

'That would be great, I'd really like that, and Mummy had the piano tuned only a couple of weeks ago so at least the notes will sound right, even if they aren't in the right order.'

We both laughed and I left her to her practice, the sounds carrying across the hallway to the bathroom and later down the stairs.

'Why didn't you tell me Sal played the flute, she's really good?' My voice was accusatory as I rounded on Jamie.

He held his hands up. 'Not down to me, she didn't want you to know. Even when we all said you'd love to play with her, she wouldn't have it, was adamant she wanted to be better before anyone said anything. Anyway, you know now so what's the problem?'

I slapped him playfully. 'The problem, young Jamie, is that she's been embarrassed all this time for no reason.' I smiled to show it wasn't a problem. 'So, are we still off to the beach today Do I need to bring anything special with me?'

'Yes and no, in that order. Just make sure you're wearing something comfortable, everything else will be in the car in no time.'

Jamie disappeared to make final arrangements and I wandered back upstairs to gather up my beach bag and slip my bikini on underneath my sun dress. The day was already hot, and the cloudless sky meant it would be hotter still by midday. I made sure I had sunscreen in my bag and knocked on Sal's door. She was just putting her flute away.

'I'm coming', she called over her shoulder, 'I'll be there in a minute, don't go without me.'

'Don't worry, there's no chance of leaving you behind Sal.' I reassured her.

Those weeks in Dorset passed peacefully. Sal and I practised regularly in the music room, taking pleasure in making music together. It was rare for me to enjoy such creativity as I normally played alone or as first violin. Taking second place to another musician was a welcome relief from the responsibility of permanent perfection.

Jamie and I found little opportunity to be alone together, and it quickly became apparent that any overnight indulgences would not only be frowned upon by the adults but would result in sanctions we may not like, so we played along with the pretence that we weren't itching to get each other's clothes off.

Despite the sexual tension between us, our relationship deepened, and we spent hours walking and talking, taking the car to far-flung beaches so we could grab a few hours without an entourage. Even at these times, we maintained our distance, sure we kissed and fumbled but we never took it any further. We agreed our first time would be special for both of us and not simply be in the back of a tiny car, legs bunched uncomfortably up around our ears.

Trips out with the rest of the family and Jamie's friends were a joy, my early insight into the pleasures of having siblings was justified and I found myself relaxing into the never-ending boisterous game of tag wherever we all happened to find ourselves.

When it was time for me to leave, I didn't want to go, but my final exam and parents beckoned. Soon, I thought, I won't be tied in this way; soon, I'll have the freedom to do what I want, when I want without being beholden to anyone else. I look back now and am amused at how naïve I was.

CHAPTER TWELVE

St Cecilia's was a revelation, a bit like summer school but without the sense of urgency. Two whole years, two years living away from home, albeit in a 'home from home' as the school brochure promised my parents.

As a senior student, I was fortunate to have my own room overlooking the rose gardens. The school was old, older than Jamieson's. It had been founded at the behest of a wealthy patron of the arts who felt St Cecilia really should have a music college of her own.

My parents had brought me, my trunk plus assorted paraphernalia including a hockey stick (one), tennis racquet (one) and violin (two, just in case one failed during a recital or concert). Mum had meticulously marked everything off the list as it was packed away ready for the beginning of term.

I was sort of helping but instead mostly mooning about, earning several rebukes to 'get cracking' and 'pull my weight and get a move on'. The latter was said with a mix of hopeless anticipation that I might actually do something but in the certain knowledge, I almost certainly wouldn't.

The summer months had dragged by since returning from the villa and I had hardly seen Jamie at all, although the letters still flew between us, and my father kept telling me he looked forward to the day he'd have the telephone to himself again.

When the time came for them to leave there were tears from my mother and a bear hug from dad. I stood on the top step watching their car as it dwindled to nothingness down the driveway.

'Hello.'

The rich country accent startled me out of my reverie. I turned around and saw a girl with a perfect complexion, long honey-coloured hair and the sweetest of smiles looking at me.

'Hello.' I replied.

'I'm Laura I've just started today too. And I saw you watching them leave, are you OK?'

Her concern was touching.

'I'm fine, I was just thinking it reminds me of summer school, but this is going to be much longer. What do you play?' As was the way with musicians, the first question was always about the instrument.

'Cello. And you?'

'Violin. Perhaps we'll be in the same classes, quartets, or something like that. Oh, and I'm Jenny by the way.' I held out my hand and she shook it solemnly.

'Nice to meet you Jenny and I've had a look at the timetable but to be honest I don't understand it. Where's your practice room?'

She was curious, I'd give her that and friendly, she seemed kind and I sensed it would be good to have a friend early on so indulged her questions. '4B I think.'

We had all been allocated a practice room, although room was probably too grand a word for it, a cubby hole was a more accurate description. 'What about you?'

She smiled back. 'Just further along from you, 7B.'

At that moment, the bell rang, and I must have looked confused.

'That's the tea bell.' She started to walk towards the entrance and then turned back to me. 'Coming?'

And so I followed.

We were almost at the end of our first year when Laura dropped her bombshell.

'Have you ever had sex Jen?' She looked at me anxiously she seemed nervous about my reply.

I was cautious in my response. 'Why do you ask?'

'I don't know, it was something you said after you saw Jamie at the weekend that made me wonder if the two of you had .. you know … done anything.'

Intuitively I knew there was more going on than her apparent awareness of my conversations with my boyfriend. 'Would it bother you if we had? Not that we have mind you.' I was careful to tell her the truth.

It was still a sore point for both of us that we still hadn't done anything more than a little light petting. I knew I was the one backing away and didn't understand why I was so reluctant to go any further. As soon as Jamie got close to anywhere near my knickers I froze.

We saw each other regularly whenever our punishing schedules allowed it. Fortunately, his university was close to St Cecilia's, and I did occasionally wonder if he had planned it that way. He would often drive over to collect me. I was the envy of the other girls, and not just because my boyfriend had a car. Jamie had filled out and grown into the looks I'd spotted when we first became a couple.

He's gorgeous they would say. You're so lucky they moaned. And I, knowing both to be facts, felt guilty that we hadn't taken it any further. I knew in my heart it had something to do with Mr Smithson but was at a loss to understand what it was.

Occasionally he would bring up the subject obliquely. 'So, when you had sex before did you do it a lot?'

And I would answer equally obliquely. 'Not so much as you'd notice.'

Sometimes it was a full-blown argument. 'Why are you like this, why can't we go all the way, we're both old enough now and you know how much I love you. You've already done it, yet I feel like the oldest virgin in town.'

His argument was valid, I knew he was saving himself for me and I couldn't, or was it wouldn't, reciprocate.

My replies were never good enough. 'I don't know Jamie. I want to, I really, really do and you know I love you too. But I freeze when you get too close and I don't know why.'

Then my tears would flow, and he would cuddle me and whisper it was OK and he was sorry for being pushy and we'd wait until it was right.

All the time I knew in my heart, it would never be right, something was broken inside me, and as I didn't know what it was how could I ever know how to fix it?

Laura looked at me and then looked away. 'I just wondered, that's all.'

'Why Laura, what's the problem?' I knew there was something she wasn't telling me and desperately wanted to help my best friend. I reached for her hand.

She looked at me and I could see she was trying to avoid answering until suddenly something inside her changed, as if her resolve had finally kicked in. 'Do you remember me telling you about my music teacher?'

I did and the way she had said it made my stomach lurch heavily.

'Yes, why?' I nodded.

'I've never told anyone this ever before so please don't repeat it, but he abused me.'

I must have looked shocked, so she repeated the request not to tell anyone else. I grasped her hand more firmly before saying. 'Of course I won't, you know that.' I was curious and wanted desperately to know if it was also Mr Smithson. 'What was his name?'

'Mr Johnson.'

Relief flooded through me leaving me light-headed and dizzy.

'Are you OK, you look like you've seen a ghost Jen?' It was Laura's turn to be concerned.

'Yes', I replied, 'I'm fine. Just shocked for you. What did you do?'

'I didn't do anything at first. He told me it was our little secret and that no one would believe me anyway because I was just a child.' She looked ready to cry and I held her hand more tightly.

'Go on'. I said.

'He made me do things, he told me it was helping me to learn to cope with anything when it came to music, and I suppose he was right in a strange way. When we go busking, what people say and do on the street, when they come up and try to make us jump or distract us it doesn't bother me in the slightest.'

My fear returned. It sounded so similar to my encounters with Mr Smithson, the man I'd barely thought of in almost two years.

'When did you decide to do something then?'

She pulled her hand away from mine and started picking at the dust on the table.

'When he said we should take it further for the music's sake. I remember just looking at him. He kept telling me to lie back on the desk, but I couldn't, I wouldn't, it was wrong, it felt all wrong. I ran out of the practice room and found another teacher. By the time he had gone to confront him, he was gone, and he disappeared from school. I haven't seen him since, and neither has anyone else.'

My face flushed as I remembered the pleasure I'd taken in lying back on the desk, being penetrated by an older man who found me sexually attractive and who called me 'beloved'. Slowly, it dawned on me that this too had been abuse, albeit of a kind that I had consented quite willingly to. I'd never thought of it in those terms before and I rolled the word 'abuse' around in my head a few times before replying.

'Why are you telling me this now Laura? What's happened, do you need some help or something?' I was concerned about her but surely if he'd left, she was no longer in any danger.

Laura looked me full in the face. 'My parents went nuts when they found out what had been going on, they only let me come here if I swore never to even look at a boy, never mind a man, again. They tried to find him, the school, and the police, but it was as if he never existed, he just vanished off the face of the earth.' She watched my face carefully. 'But then I saw him again, last week when we were performing. He was in the audience, watching and I was pretty sure it was him, even though he'd changed a lot.'

I knew enough about panic to try and keep her calm. 'Have you told anyone what you saw Laura, did you report it to one of the teachers here?'

'Yes.' She nodded her head to emphasise the point. 'Yes, I did, but by the time they got to the auditorium he was gone, and I couldn't remember what he looked like so they all thought I was seeing things.'

She looked down. 'You do believe me though, don't you Jenny?'

I picked up her hand again how could I say no, I knew what she was going through. 'Yes, yes of course I do Laura.'

CHAPTER THIRTEEN

Jamie and Jenny had left for the station. Davey was in his room reading and her parents were working in the estate office. Sally scuffed her feet not sure what to do with herself now her musical companion had left.

Sighing, she looked out at the garden.

Meeting friends was an option. Ciara had said they were going to the beach with their bikes and did she want to come. She'd said no at the time, but perhaps it was better than moping around with nothing to do.

St Cecilia's beckoned but there was still another week to go before starting her new school. A week of getting ready, packing and everything else that entailed. Jenny had already moved on to university but would be close by, like Jamie.

Retrieving her bike from the sheds at the side of the house she poked her head around the door of the estate office.

'I'm meeting Ciara and the others down at the beach. I've got some money and I'll get some lunch from the café.' She didn't bother asking, she was merely informing them of her whereabouts as agreed.

Her mother nodded. 'Take care on the lanes darling and don't be back too late, we've got guests coming to dinner.'

Nodding, Sally backed out of the door and headed off down the drive at a lick.

It was a glorious day, one that made you feel it would never rain again. The sun was bright against the sharp blue sky, the air smelt musty and the leaves were ready to turn, a sure sign of summer's closing. It was always like that at this time of year she reflected, the bright freshness of spring greens, giving way to a dustier, darker, dirtier green as the summer progressed and plants struggled in the heat.

Thirty minutes of hard cycling, and she was in the car park. Scanning the length of the beach she looked for the pack that indicated her friends. Spotting them in the distance she chained her bike alongside Ciara's and trudged up along the shingle beach to meet them.

Ciara spotted her first. 'I thought you were too busy to come out?' Her tone was accusatory.

'I changed my mind, thought it would be nice to while away an hour or two baking in the sun with my best friend,' Sally smiled. 'After all I'm going to be away for six weeks soon'.

Joe called out. 'Hey Sal, I thought you weren't coming'.

'I was just saying I changed my mind.' She could see he was holding something delicately in his hands. 'What are you doing?'

Crawling closer she saw it was a fish, still flapping feebly in the air.

'One of the fishermen didn't throw it back far enough and I spotted it on the shoreline. I'm going to put it back.' He wandered down to the water's edge. Sally followed him, pulling off her tee shirt as she went.

She watched him wade out to his waist and gently lay the fish in the water. For a few moments, it didn't move, and her heart was in her mouth, perhaps it had died after all; then suddenly, it flipped its tail and was gone, silver scales flashing brightly in the sunlight.

Joe waded back to shore and shading his eyes, looked at her.

'How have you been?' He asked it lightly. The previous year they had been a sort of couple for a few weeks, but school breaks spent in France since had put paid to any burgeoning romance.

'OK.' she said. 'You?'

'Yeah, I'm OK too.' He smiled. 'Race you back to the others.' And sprinted off.

Sally took her time, flopping down on the shingle next to Ciara, who raised the edge of her hat to look at her properly. 'Hello again.'

Slipping off her shorts and discarding the teeshirt she was carrying, Sally laid back in the warmth too and shading her eyes with her hand wished she'd had the foresight to bring a hat or sunglasses too.

Stretching out a hand she hunted around in her bag for sun lotion and began smearing it on all the exposed bits. It wouldn't do to be burnt at this stage of the holidays.

Turning over she undid the straps of her halter neck top. 'Joe, could you put some cream on my back pretty please?' This was pushing it and she knew he might just say no.

But he didn't. Instead, he sidled over good-naturedly asking 'So what did your last slave die of?'

It felt good to have his hands rub the cool cream into her skin and she relaxed into the massage. When he had finished, he lay down propping himself up on one arm next to both girls. The rest of the group was playing a slow game of tag, but it was far too energetic for a hot summer's day.

Sally was aware of his presence, and she could feel his eyes looking at her.

'What?'

'Nothing' he replied. 'Just looking'.

She was mildly amused. 'And do you like what you see?'

'Of course, Ciara is gorgeous, and you're not so bad yourself'.

Ciara opened one eye. 'For god's sake get over yourselves. Get a room and leave me in peace.'

Joe flopped down on his back and snaked his hand across the sand towards Sally. He pinched her lightly on the side and she jumped.

'Ouch, that hurt.' She accused with mock outrage, secretly enjoying the latent interest. They hadn't taken it any further than a kiss and a quick fumble in her bra, but that didn't mean she hadn't wanted to experiment. Sally wondered if he felt the same, it wasn't something they talked about, surrounded as they were most of the time by friends or family.

'Stop complaining.' He admonished her but he pulled his hand away and they lay quietly.

Sally woke with a start she must have drifted off in the warmth.

'Who's that bloke over there? He's been watching us for ages?' Ciara pointed over to the car park and everyone turned around to look. The man, aware of their stares turned on his heel and walked off to the far side of the car park.

'Just some perv Ciara.' One of the other boys said. 'He's gone now and anyway, we're here to protect you.' They all laughed.

At lunchtime, they trooped over to the café for chips and coke.

'I really should eat something healthy.' Sally screwed her face up at the chips she was eating. 'But I can't be bothered, and it doesn't seem to matter much.' She stroked her flat belly.

'You're so lucky.' Chimed Fi. 'You can eat anything, I put weight on just thinking about food.' They all laughed, even Fi as her love of food, and chocolate in particular was legendary and her figure was voluptuous. She was going to be the beauty of the group they all agreed.

After lunch, they pooled the remains of their money and gathered up a supply of fizzy drinks and sweets to take back to their preferred spot on the beach. As they left the café, Ciara noticed the man again.

'Look he's still here.' She said. 'The man watching us earlier'. She pulled a face. 'He's creepy and it's making my skin crawl.'

Sally, looked over at the bloke who just stood there watching them, wondering what he was doing. She had the strangest sense of recognition, that he was familiar in some way and that he was watching her specifically. She shivered and pulled on her tee shirt.

Putting herself right in the middle of the group she ventured a look back, but he seemed to have disappeared.

The afternoon passed in a haze of laughter as they indulged in game after game of swimming tag. The object of the game was to jump on unsuspecting members of the group and push them under. By the time they were finished, they were all tired, had sand in their hair and were ready to head for home.

Cycling up the lane was much harder than heading down to the sea Sally thought as she trailed the others ahead of her. They all headed off in different directions when they reached the village, shouting out meeting arrangements for the following day.

The day had turned, and the wind had got up, just in time for the evening. It was pleasant cycling the lanes back home and Sally was in a state of blissful reverie when a car horn blasted out of nowhere. She was so surprised she fell off her bike hitting the ground hard right next to a dense hedge.

Dazed, she sat up wondering what on earth had happened and saw a car parked just ahead of her in the layby on the bend.

The driver looked oddly familiar and with a start, she realised it was the man from the beach. So that was why he looked familiar, she'd noticed the car parked in the same place several times over the last few weeks, but had never given it much thought; the layby was often used by walkers.

Wondering what he was doing and why he had sounded the horn she picked up her bike resolving to mention the incident to her parents. Instinctively she knew something wasn't quite right but couldn't quite put her finger on it.

Looking at her bike she saw the chain had come loose in the fall and sighed heavily, she'd have to push it the rest of the way and ask one of the groundsmen to fix it for her.

As she was preparing to carry on her way, a shadow fell across her and she shrank away. Turning she noticed the man had come close, so close she could smell his cigarette and coffee breath. She screwed her face up in revulsion, and as she did so he smiled; not one that was nice and welcoming, it was predatory and momentarily she was reminded of the wolf and red riding hood.

'What do you want?' Her voice did not come out as strongly as she had hoped.

He never said anything, just took the bike from her and began pushing it in the direction of the house, she followed mutely, not quite sure what was going on, but as they were heading towards home played along with it.

As he drew level with the farm gate on the other side of the lane he stopped and looked back, then wheeled her bike over to the gate, opened it and pushed it through.

'Hey, what are you doing that's my bike?' He ignored her and carried on through the gate and round the back of the hedge, disappearing.

Sally followed him wondering what he could want with her bike. She wanted to run home but was prevented from doing so for fear of what her parents would say when she told them she had let it be taken.

Rushing through the gate she strained to see where he had gone but there was no one there. A flash of blue caught her eye along the line of hedgerow so she walked quickly in the furrow driven by late ploughing.

The copse at the field boundary was dense with undergrowth with a few trees surrounding a small pond. Pushing her way through the branches she was momentarily blinded as she closed her eyes to avoid the sharp branches springing back at her. Arms out in front, she pushed out into a small clearing, but before she could make sense of her surroundings, he grabbed her right arm and pulled her roughly in front of him, clamping a hand over her mouth at the same time.

Struggling, she pulled back against him, but he had the advantage. He was muscular and held her easily. She sagged hoping to get an opportunity to break free if he stumbled, but his footing was sure, as if he knew the way.

Sally's eyes darted about trying to work out in her head where he was herding her. Vague recollections of a small tumbledown barn appeared in her mind's eye. It wasn't somewhere they ever went; this land didn't belong to her family and a long-ago feud had put paid to any adventuring.

She pulled vainly against the strength of his grip.

'Stop struggling, it'll be much easier for us both.' His voice was oddly melodic and quietly spoken, nevertheless she heard the implied threat and sagged down.

He hauled her up. 'Walk.' He commanded.

She put one foot in front of the other in the direction he pushed her. Every fibre of her being wanted to resist yet knowing if she did so the consequences, when they came, might be dire.

Eventually, they reached the old barn and he kicked open the door with his foot pushing her roughly inside. She fell heavily and landed on a heap of straw. Rolling over she was about to scream when his hands were around her mouth again. She bit down strongly, and he pulled them off quickly.

'Bitch.' He spat and slapped her. 'Try that again and you really will have something to scream about'.

Grabbing her again, he pulled off a piece of black masking tape that had been placed ready and strapped it over her mouth. She could hardly breathe and fearing she would faint started to pant through her nose instead.

She reached up to pull the tape off her mouth and he grabbed her arms again.

'No, that's not going to happen.' He whispered in her ear. 'You and I are going to have some fun, but I'd like you to enjoy it. Do you think you could enjoy it?' His question confused her, what could she possibly find to enjoy in this, but sensing his eyes on her she nodded quickly.

'OK, I'm going to let go of your arms. But don't try anything, I'll always be faster than you and I've prepared well Sally.'

His use of her name stilled her. How did he know who she was? Had he been following her? The feeling she'd had at the beach, that he was there for her came flooding back and her fear intensified.

He pushed her roughly back onto the straw and headed back to the barn door. Pushing it closed, a heavy bar completed the lock. She was a prisoner.

The man walked back slowly, like a cat stalking its prey she thought, and Sally shuffled back further into the bales. He smiled, the same feline look of earlier and she turned her face away.

'Come now Sally, don't be like that.' He cajoled. 'I said we'd have some fun. I don't want to hurt you just educate you.' He took her face gently and turned it round, his breath faster now, stung her nose.

'You must be wondering who I am?'

She nodded, wondering where it was all going.

'My name is Mr Smithson; you can call me Mr Smithson.' Appraising her carefully, he looked her over from all angles. 'Stand up Sally.'

She stood.

'Now hold up your arms'.

She held her arms up and he removed her tee-shirt. She kept them up.

'Put them down Sally, you don't need to suffer.'

He turned her round and undid the ties of her bikini top; it fell to the ground and she instinctively went to cover her breasts.

He grabbed her hands again. 'No, no, no, Sally. Don't be shy. I just want to look at you for a moment. You have beautiful breasts, sweet and juicy and …' he paused '.. ready for plucking'.

'Lie down Sally.' He gently pushed her down and laid her back on the straw.

Unable to do anything, her mind closed off, and she drifted off to the meadow she had played in with Jamie and Davey when they were children. She could not face what was happening to her, and so she left.

Hours later she came too. Voices calling roused her. It was dark and she was alone. Fumbling with the tape on her mouth she pulled it off and called out weakly.

A flashlight flooded the barn and she shied away from the strong arms that reached for her naked body.

Then her mother was there, cradling her gently and stroking her head, pushing back the hair as she had when she was a child.

'My darling, my darling.' Her mother crooned over and over again.

She was given strong tea with sugar and biscuits, forcing them down even though she didn't want them.

Sat in the drawing room Sally tried to recount what had happened to the policemen who listened but it was all a jumble and large parts were missing from her memory. Every time she recalled being pushed back on the straw she wept fresh tears, their hot saltiness mingling with the taste of cigarettes and coffee in her mouth.

No, she didn't know who he was. No, she didn't know what make his car was, except it was red and small. No, she didn't know his name. No, no, no. To every question, she answered No.

Later, in the dead of night, the name returned, and she turned it over in her memory, Mr Smithson. She knew it wasn't his name, just one he had plucked out of thin air to confuse her, so she never shared it.

Over the next weeks, the police investigation ground to a halt. They couldn't find any evidence of the man, and her friend's descriptions had varied so much that an identikit was almost impossible.

Her family treated her like a China doll until she could stand it no longer and she demanded to see her friends. Friends who looked at her differently, were no longer as free and easy with her as they had once been, friends who didn't know what to say. And particular friends like Joe who she was now certain saw her as damaged goods; so she retreated from them as well.

Her brothers were solicitous. 'If I ever catch the bastard who did this, I'll kill him.' said Jamie.

'Hanging would be too good for a man like that.' Davey agreed.

Both knew their little sister needed protecting, and each vowed to do what they could to establish recompense for the trauma she had suffered.

Her flute became her safety net. An inanimate object providing solace that never asked any questions she couldn't answer, wouldn't answer. She played long into the night, haunting melodies that spoke of the pain she had endured and the hope she saw in the future. Her family listened, lying awake in their beds, unable to reach her or answer her constant question; why?

Sally began at St Cecilia's a month later than intended. The quiet sanctity of the college soothed her soul and she relaxed into the routine and life away from home far better than many of her peers.

Animated, she threw herself into college life signing up to anything and everything, keeping her mind on other things and away from the dark thoughts that pervaded her wakefulness. When she slept, which was rare, it was to face dreams she woke from sweating and panting. Dreams of lust and violence that both repelled and enticed her in ways she didn't understand, didn't want to understand.

Her mother hadn't wanted her to go, but her father understood her need to regain herself after her ordeal and forced it through. All the while he reminded her she could return home if it became too much, that they would always be here for her, and that it was her strength that would see her through.

Leaving her past behind was, she decided, the best thing she could do to get over what had happened, and she embraced the opportunity with an optimism she didn't feel, and a smile that rarely reached her eyes.

CHAPTER FOURTEEN

'Stop it Tom'. I threw a cushion at him laughing. 'Stop it, you're making my stomach hurt. It's too much. You've got to stop with the bad jokes.'

He gave me his fake puppy dog look. 'But you lurve me, you lurve me .. and you lurve my jokes too, tell me you love my jokes too otherwise I think I'll have to kill myself and it will be all your fault. You'll have to break the news to my family when they haul my poor broken body from the bottom of the nearest river.'

I laughed. 'Oh alright then, I'll lurve the jokes too.' And kissed him while I pulled on warm jeans and sweatshirt.

'Come on, it's time to go. I've got to go practice and you've got a dissertation to finish.' I was firm but fair.

I was heartless when it came to throwing him out, nothing got between me and my violin. The auditions for associate members of some of the country's greatest orchestras were starting in just a couple of weeks, and I had no intention of not being selected by at least two.

Tom pulled on his jeans and threw his tee-shirt over his shoulder and made for the door calling 'later babes' and was gone.

I stood for a moment in the middle of my room and considered clearing up. I thought better of it, I'll leave it till I get back I thought to myself grabbing my violin and pulling the door closed behind me.

I met Laura outside the practice halls, she was just leaving and looked at me archly. 'You'll never get in if you keep spending all your time with the gorgeous Tom you know.'

I smiled. 'He knows which side of the bread has butter on and wouldn't dare come between me and my practice.'

She laughed. 'Coffee catch up later?'

'Yes please.' I called over my shoulder. 'I'll see you about 1 o'clock in the usual place.' And headed off to my cubby hole. Unlocking the door, I pushed past a pile of sheet music and opened the blinds. The light was streaming in from the South, and I was half-minded to close them when memories of being in a darkened practice room with a man I thought was my friend came flooding back.

Laura's revelation three years earlier had precipitated a deep depression in me. I'd revisited my past so often in those first few months after our conversation it bordered on obsession and, when eventually I confessed what had happened to Jamie, he was rocked to his core.

'I can't believe you never told me, I can't believe you thought it was OK. In fact, I can't believe anything you say any more.' The arguments spiralled out of control, becoming more regular and more ferocious.

At the heart of it was Jamie's pride and my guilt. He thought he wasn't good enough because I couldn't make love with him. I felt guilty because I'd enjoyed what had happened with Mr Smithson and was torn between feeling it had been so right when it was really so wrong.

Reviewing every event, every nuance, every conversation, and every practice session made me understand I had always been the prey; that it had been a deliberate act of abuse by a controlling and manipulative paedophile. But I felt guilty of complicity. In my head was the belief I had actively encouraged him so how could I in truth, say he was wholly to blame?

When I told Laura what had happened to me, she asked me why I'd never said anything, and I struggled to explain all I felt. I still couldn't tell anyone else. The only people who knew were Jamie, Laura and of course, Mr Smithson. It was a secret I was never going to share elsewhere if I could help it.

Jamie didn't cope well with my revelations and by the time I'd finished my first year at Uni we had drifted apart. Here I was, at the same University he attended and in all that time our paths rarely crossed. When they did, he smiled and was his usual kind and generous self, but that was as far as it went, and my heart ached for his love.

I'd fallen into a series of flings, none of which meant anything. They were a useful distraction from the pain of losing the man I loved. The latest was Tom, he'd been around about four months, and I was already wondering if it was time to move on again.

Sex became a way to patch a broken heart and cover up my maimed self. It was good, it was always good. I'd been taught by the best and knew how to give and receive pleasure in equal measure. But, as soon as it became something more than fun then I needed to get out, get away and move on. I couldn't cope with the closeness of love when my heart and mind were still full of Jamie and the love we'd never been able to consummate.

With my heartache in mind, I lifted my violin and raised it to my neck. Starting with the Canon in D, my favourite piece and the one that always stilled my roiling tempestuous thoughts.

By the last refrain, I was calm and began to work my way through the other pieces I was working on. Some didn't sound quite right as they were orchestral and the violin was just another instrument and I could, if I wanted, skip between different instrumental parts creating something unique that only I would ever hear.

Finally, I finished with scales. Most students began with them to warm up, but I always used them as a warm down, a way of saying goodnight to my violin before putting it to bed for the next few hours.

I looked at the clock on the wall, ten to one. I had just enough time to take my case back to my room before meeting Laura for coffee. I raced over the quad and climbed the stairs two at a time and was just about to put the key in my door when someone called my name.

'Jenny, is that you Jenny?'

I turned around and saw Sally standing at the far end of the corridor.

'Sal, what on earth are you doing here?' I couldn't keep the note of concern out of my voice as it had been almost three years since I'd seen her, she didn't look good.

'I've just started Jenny and it's taken me a couple of months to work up the courage to come and say hello. After you and Jamie split up it didn't seem right somehow.' She looked at me hopefully.

I looked at her. 'I'm just going to meet Laura for a coffee, you remember Laura, don't you?'

She nodded and I carried on. 'Why don't you come with me and then you and I can catch up properly later.'

'Oh, yes please, I'd like that, thank you.' Sal's face lit up as she smiled and the darkness around her eyes lifted, just a little.

Laura was not best pleased to see Sal with me, giving me a sidelong look and raising her eyes in exasperation. It was soon apparent she had news to impart.

'He was there again.' She didn't need to say who 'he' was, we both knew she was talking about Mr Johnson. 'Sat in the middle, plain as day and looking like the cat that got the cream.'

This had become a regular occurrence whenever she performed, and it was very unnerving for her.

She had spoken to the head at St Cecilia's and later to the heads of music and pastoral care at the university, but all had said that a man turning up to watch performances by students didn't mean there was anything sinister going on, their hands were tied unless she could offer them something else.

Laura, like me, didn't want to divulge her part in the situation with Mr Johnson. Guilt played a large part in her life too. After all, how could she, an intelligent girl with a way above-average IQ have let someone manipulate her the way he had done? Shame would course across her features every time she talked about it, and I understood every bit of it.

'It's not as if we were little kids, we had a choice.' She looked askance, 'Didn't we?'

I wanted to reassure her and say of course we did. But in my heart, I was beginning to wonder whether that was truly the case and what the outcome might have been had we resisted or told someone, anyone.

I held her hand. 'Can you ignore him?'

I asked it, knowing the answer she would give me even before she replied. We'd had this conversation many times over the last three years and this one would be no different.

She was not best pleased. 'Don't you think I try to do that at every performance, it's not as if he didn't teach me well enough.'

Sal looked confused.

'Don't worry it's just a bloke that's annoying Laura a lot at the moment, he won't go away.' I explained.

She nodded as if she understood, but I knew she didn't, wouldn't, couldn't.

Laura rounded on me. 'Annoying, you think this is annoying. Annoying is getting a stone in your shoe, annoying is hitting a bum note in practice.

This.' Her voice getting shriller and louder. 'is NOT ANNOYING. This is creepy and I'm frightened.'

She sat back in her seat and glared at me across the coffee cups.

'I'm sorry.' I said. 'I shouldn't have belittled it like that, I do understand honest.' I held my hands out in supplication. 'Friends?'

She took my hands and smiled sadly. 'Friends.' She affirmed. 'But I am frightened Jenny, I'm frightened for what he might do next.'

Throughout the exchange Sal just sat and stared at both of us, looking more confused with each bit of the conversation.

'Can I catch you later Jenny?' She asked 'I think I probably need to leave you two to yourselves.'

'Thanks Sal.' I smiled at her gratefully. 'That would probably be better. You know where I am now so knock on the door any time after seven tonight and I'll be there.'

Sal waved as she left the coffee shop and I waved back before turning my attention back to Laura.

'We could always try the police again.' I offered.

She looked at me. 'What would be the point of that? Unless I'm prepared to reveal all the gory details and my part in the whole sordid mess, they'll say they can't do anything. And I can't do that I don't want people to see me as a slapper.'

I knew what she meant, the same worries and concerns held me back from telling other people my story too. The reaction from Jamie had been enough to make sure I would never let anyone else look at me with disgust again.

'We'll figure something out eventually. In the meantime, you must be strong. I know you are, and I know you'll get through this.' I sounded more positive than I felt. 'Come on, let's go and practice together, that'll take our minds off it for a while and you never know, we might just hit on a solution.'

I pulled her out of her seat, and we walked, arm in arm back to our rooms, collected our instruments and headed for the practice hall.

'Your cubby or mine?' I asked.

'Yours definitely, it's less messy than mine.' She replied with a smile.

Playing with Laura was always a pleasure. And because we both knew the other's secret, we didn't have to hide the effect playing had on either of us. We sighed and relaxed in unison as the notes washed over us, cleansing our minds and our bodies.

'We should do this more often, it's always a joy playing with you Laura.'

We rarely played together as we were in different classes and orchestras. The idea as far as the music school was concerned was to ease the load of professional performances for all students. It did mean that we only played together at the biggest events, like Christmas and end-of-year festivals. But even then we might not play on the same day or even in the same location.

The closest we came to playing regularly was busking in the city centre in the run-up to Christmas when a group of us would get together and spend a few chilly Saturdays playing for shoppers and staff alike.

'It would be a bit odd, a violin and a cello, we'd need more than that to play together.' She laughed.

I had to agree, we'd need more than just the two of us.

'Let's think about it anyway, neither of us are doing anything else at the moment what with these auditions coming up, but hey – you never know.'

I pushed the idea to the back of my mind and concentrated on packing up.

Seven o'clock came and went and there was no sign of Sal, so I headed over to Tom's hall.

'Hey you.' I said when he opened the door. 'You want to put a poor girl up for the night?' I winked and lifted my leg as if turning a trick.

Laughing, he pulled me into a rough hug and kissed me thoroughly.

'I'd do anything for a girl like you.' He leered at me. 'Come into my lair and I'll ravish you'.

Giggling I went to the window to close the curtains against the night. At first, I thought I was seeing things, I looked again and sure enough, there was a familiar figure standing looking right up at me from underneath the street light. I closed the curtains quickly, my heart beating fast and my hands shaking. Mr Smithson, the voice in my head shouted the name so loudly I thought Tom might hear, but he was too busy pouring beer into glasses to notice.

What on earth was he doing out there, had he followed me? It was the only conclusion I could reach. I pulled the curtains aside a little to look out again. He was gone!

My first thought was I must have imagined it. My second was not to be so stupid, the brain plays tricks and the conversation with Laura had heightened my awareness so much it was making me see things.

I turned to Tom and smiled brightly to cover my nerves.

'So, what delights have you got in store for this poor waif and stray tonight Mr Jones?'

He almost smacked his lips as he handed me a glass.

'Just get that on down you little lady and we'll see.'

I took the glass and drank the contents in one go.

'Hey not so fast Jen, I've only got a couple of bottles and they're supposed to last the night. It's not as if I've got money to burn you know.'

He whipped the empty glass out of my hand and put it out of reach.

'You're going to have to earn the next one.'

I took the glass out of his hand and put it on his desk then pulled him over to the bed.

'I don't know what it is about you Jen, but you're like no one I've ever come across before.'

He raised himself on one arm and stroked my belly gently.

'Will you tell me your secret?'

I turned my head away. That was never going to happen, and the moment was spoilt.

Sitting up, I said 'I have to go.'

He looked confused. 'You've only just got here, I thought you were staying. I could do this all night.' He leered at me and tried to grab a nipple, but I turned away, momentarily disgusted with myself and him.

'No, sorry, my mistake I've just remembered I've got loads of work to finish off before the end of the week.'

I pulled on my knickers. Their cold, smelly wetness made me cringe, but I dragged my jeans over them and locked it away. Grabbing my tee-shirt, I looked back at him lying on the bed and half smiled.

'See you tomorrow then babe.'

It wasn't a question, more an assumption he made.

'I'm not sure, I'll see how I get on with my work.'

In my head, I knew I wouldn't see him again. It had gone too far, again.

'Bye Tom.' I said and closed the door gently behind me.

I leaned back against the cool corridor wall and thought about what had just happened. Since Jamie, there had been a few like Tom. I could be a slut, a whore and enjoy sex in its rawest forms. But there came a point with everyone where they wanted to know more about me and what had made me the girl of their dreams.

Slowly it dawned on me I was acting out. This wasn't me, but it was all I knew sex to be. Somehow, somewhere along the way I'd become a caricature of myself, pliable to another's needs and wants. Allowing them to see themselves through me, being whoever, it was they wanted and as sexy as they seemed to need.

I reflected that apart from orgasm I didn't even enjoy it all that much. All the thrusting, panting, groaning, and words shouted out were just nonsense before they cut to the chase and brought me back to heel.

My mind drifted back to Mr Smithson wondering what I'd actually seen in the darkness outside Tom's room. I reflected that perhaps it was my earlier review of past events and the way I'd recast them in my mind that was causing me to see things.

I could see the link now between how I was with Tom and how I'd been as that gawky, shy teenager groomed by an older man to be a sexual puppet.

It disgusted me, I disgusted me. It was no wonder Jamie had left me. I could no more be the girlfriend of someone as good as he was when I had no morals to speak of.

Tears pricked my eyes and I wiped them away furiously before heading back to my room. Warily, I found myself looking over my shoulder every few minutes in case the phantasm of Mr Smithson loomed out of the darkness to finally consume me.

When I got back, I discovered a note from Sal tacked to the noticeboard on my door.

'Sorry, I got caught up with stuff and was late. Can we meet up tomorrow, please? I'll be at the same café about 11ish if you're free. Thanks, Sal x.'

'I've got no lectures at the moment as we're all working towards the orchestral auditions.' I explained when I met her the next day. 'So how are you, what have you been doing all this time and are you still playing?' My questions came out in a rush, I wanted to know everything.

'I'm fine, I think. And yes, I'm still playing flute. I'm studying music here.' She looked at me.

'I think, Sal, what does that mean?' I asked, referring to her first statement.

'Well, you know, things and stuff, it's not always plain sailing is it, life you know?'

I nodded in agreement, 'You're right there Sal.'

Pausing, I asked a passing waitress for a coffee, black with no sugar. It had been the same order for almost eight years, and I never varied. I no longer thought about the reason why, but the memory lingered of my first sip of coffee and its relationship to forbidden fruit.

'Is Jamie OK?' I tried to keep my voice light, and friendly, rather than the desperation I felt.

'He's fine.' Her clear look said more, and I smiled.

'He misses you.' She said it simply. 'He doesn't realise it, but the whole family can tell.'

'I miss him too Sal, very much and I was really sad when we split up.' I admitted.

'So, what happened between you two? One minute you were all lovey dovey and the next, kaput, it was all over?' She waved her hands in the air to emphasise the point.

'Oh, you know, stuff, that thing called life, it just got in the way of us really.' I didn't go into details, if she didn't know then Jamie hadn't said anything, and I wasn't going to change that.

I asked the question most frequently on my mind 'Is he seeing anyone?'

Looking at me appraisingly she replied with a shake of her head. 'Not at the moment, and anyone he has seen doesn't last two minutes. Perhaps you two should catch up again?'

'Oh, I don't think that would be a good idea Sal, it wasn't great when we split, and we both said things that maybe we can't go back from.'

I looked away hoping she wouldn't notice the tears forming. To see and be with Jamie again would be so good, but it was impossible with the knowledge that stood between us.

'Ah well, at least I tried. I can tell him that much anyway.'

'You mean he knew you were catching up with me?' I could hardly keep the hope out of my voice.

'Of course, why wouldn't he?' She was curious. 'He was the one who suggested you'd be happy to see me and give me some hints and tips about university life.'

My heart soared, Jamie still thought about me enough to suggest his little sister find me.

'That sounds such a good idea Sal.'

At that moment, I'd have sold my soul to her just to prove him right. Perhaps there could be hope after all. My spirits rose significantly so I suggested a second coffee for both of us.

'Sorry, I can't, I've got to get back for a lecture.' And with that Sal was out of her seat and heading off saying 'We can catch up again later in the week if you're available, I'll leave a note on your door with my timetable and my room number, so whenever suits you will suit me too.'

She waved as she headed out the door.

I sat for a few moments, unsure what to do next. I ordered another coffee and nursed it while I turned over the latest surprising revelation in my head. My world had just shifted on its axis yet again, this time it felt like it was spinning in a more positive direction, and I smiled.

CHAPTER FIFTEEN

With a cello firmly between her legs and her bow poised, she was ready to begin. The conductor lifted his baton, and the first violin began. Laura watched the score unfold before her and in the moment before she needed to strike the right note she lifted her bow and bent forward. The bow pulled slightly as she drew it across the strings and there was a slightly discordant tone, she winced and quickly glanced around. Fortunately, no one else had noticed and the conductor, playing more for the audience than for the guidance of the musicians carried on as if nothing had happened.

She relaxed and the music flowed more easily. No need to worry, no need to be concerned that he might be in the audience, no need to think about him at all. She was safe here, amongst her classmates, family and friends. He couldn't touch her, he could only ever just watch from the sidelines.

When she left it would be in a group, giggling and laughing at the bar to mingle with the audience and talk about music and other things. She was never alone.

Jenny was right, she usually was, she reflected. He couldn't hurt her, and she was hurting herself by letting him get to her. Better to show him he was nothing, meant nothing and she didn't care about what had happened in the past, the only thing that mattered was now.

'Hey Laura.' Jenny called over from the bar waving a glass in the air. 'What are you drinking?'

'Just a large glass of water right now, I'm parched from holding my breath when I went wrong. I was so sure everyone would notice, did you?'

Jenny laughed, 'Only because it was written all over your face idiot. I'd have had no idea either if I hadn't noticed that.'

She handed over a pint of water and ice and continued drinking her own pint of shandy.

'Was he there?' Jenny asked the question carefully; she didn't want to stir up muddy water unless it was absolutely necessary.

Laura looked uncomfortable. 'Yes, about six rows in front of you at the side, didn't you see him?'

Jenny grimaced. 'Sorry Lau, I didn't. I did look around but it's dark out there and not easy to see other people when the lights go down.'

She didn't add that Laura's description had been rather vague, and she hadn't spotted any single men. It seemed to her the auditorium was filled with couples, groups of friends and the student's families.

'Anyway.' She said brightly. 'Here's to another stunning performance from the amazing Laura Best. You were fab up there you know and you looked so ..' She struggled to find the right word for it. 'So .. confident and professional, that's it, you looked like you could have stepped off the stage with the Phil like you belonged.'

Grabbing Laura's free hand. 'You're going to be so successful; you do know that don't you?'

Laura blushed, she was unused to compliments, preferring instead to hear harsh criticism; somehow it was easier to take than praise.

'Thanks Jenny, it's good to have a friend like you.' And she squeezed her hand back.

'I've finished my water and I'm going to do the bar battle do you want another drink J?' Laura got out of her seat.

Jenny shook her head, 'No thanks, I've had two already and I've got an early class tomorrow, so I'll nurse this one a bit longer.'

Laura fought through the crowd, stopping every so often to be congratulated by other students and friends on her performance. The words, amazing, fab, and brilliant all clung to her like glue and by the time she got her drink and had pushed back through the crowd to Jenny, she was glowing.

'Wow, did I do that well tonight?' She was incredulous and her head swam with the praise.

'Yep, you did do that well Laura.'

Jenny softened her look. 'It worked then? Ignoring him, putting him in the compartment marked irrelevant?'

Laura looked down and nodded.

'You were right, you know, being able to put it all to one side was sort of freeing. I don't know if I can describe it any other way, but I felt .. lighter .. somehow. I could see him sitting there, staring at me, but he had lost his power and..' She paused '.. It felt like I was sticking two fingers up at him.'

'Well get you.' Jenny was impressed, it seemed her best friend was finally getting over the horror of Mr Johnson.

Jenny stood up. 'I have to go Laura; do you want to walk back with me?'

Laura shook her head. 'No it's OK, I'm meeting up with Rob and he'll walk me back. Fortunately, I don't have to get up so early tomorrow because I'm not studying some obscure ancient music like some I can name.'

Jenny slapped her on the arm painfully. 'Get away with you, you know that's only because your latest beau just happened to be doing modern jazz instead.' She smiled. 'See you tomorrow then, for coffee?'

Laura nodded, 'OK, I'll be done with practice by 11.00 and I'll see you then.'

Laura followed Jenny through the crowd looking out for Rob, spotting him in a corner with their usual crowd. She wandered over and snaked her arm around his waist. 'Hello, you.'

He kissed her lightly on the head put an arm protectively around her shoulders and continued the heated debate he was engaged in.

She stood, warm in his embrace, listening to the good-natured banter moving backwards and forwards amongst the group. She didn't feel any need to join in and was content to bask in the performance afterglow, steadying her internal metronome to a slower, more normal beat.

Finally, the debate concluded, and Rob turned to her. 'Bed?'

It was just one word, and she smiled, nodding.

Their lovemaking was a slow, languorous affair. It began the same way it always did, with him slowly peeling off her clothes, layer by layer until she was revealed in the moonlight, like Aphrodite in the oyster. He smiled and stroked her shoulders until she shivered.

Climbing into his bed, she watched him as he took off his tee shirt, jeans, and boxers.

'Looking good Rob, looking good.' She winked at him suggestively and he jumped on her, making her squeal.

'Get off me, you're flipping heavy you great lump.' Wriggling over in the single bed she gave him enough room to climb in beside her and they snuggled down underneath the weight of sheets and blankets.

'It's not that warm Rob, warm me up.' She murmured.

And he took her hands, one by one and gently rubbed them until they glowed, putting each one between his legs when he was done.

She wriggled down the bed leaving her hands where they were as he kissed her gently, on the nose, and both cheeks, her lips full and red, and then moving slowly down her body to her neck and collarbone.

This was the bit she loved the most, the antithesis of being pushed, prodded, and pulled by Mr Johnson. Laura's thoughts lingered, just for a moment, on the memory of the day she ran away and then moved on, focusing on what Rob was doing to her body. The sensations his touch was arousing in her and how her body unbidden, rose to the challenge.

He moaned softly. 'God Laura, you are so amazing. What did I ever do to deserve a girlfriend like you?'

It was a rhetorical question she never needed to answer instead she wrapped her leg over the top of his to pull him closer.

Afterwards, she left, she always left. She couldn't stand to share her night-time with anyone other than herself.

'Will I see you tomorrow, Laura?' His voice was plaintive. He knew better than to ask as she was as likely to say no as yes. Sometimes, he wouldn't see her for days at a time when she got a bee in her bonnet about needing her own space.

'Maybe Rob, maybe'. I'll let you know.' and with that, she was gone.

Back in her room, she relaxed. The release that sex brought from her demons was just that, release but not forgiveness. It was temporary, transient She had yet to work out how to overcome them completely.

She went to the bathroom it was late and there was no one else about so she could have the bath to herself for hours if she wanted. She swished her hand through the water as it ran, waiting for it to fill so she could sink into and under it.

It was always the same. The crescendo and then a crash back to earth. Water soothed her frazzled emotions, and she would lie like the lady of the lake for hours sometimes when there was no one around, topping up the water when it grew too cold; her thoughts swirling around her like a dense fog she couldn't escape from.

Laura was reflective, her performance this time had been different. Apart from the stupid mistake at the beginning even she had to acknowledge it was the best she had ever played. He'd taught her well, she just had to take the lessons in and replay them back again. Never minding what was going on outside, just what was happening with the music inside; that was the important thing, that was what mattered.

He, wherever he was, was an irrelevance, a blot on her internal landscape she couldn't erase and perhaps, after all, it was a blot that shouldn't be removed. This was a new thought and Laura mulled it over, turning it this way and that. Could her experience make her a better musician? Could his abuse of her be turned toward something positive?

An hour later, with the question unresolved in her mind she climbed out of the bath, dried herself and headed back to her room.

Turning the light out, she opened the curtains and looked out.

There he was, where he always was after she had performed. Underneath the streetlight looking straight up at her.

He knows, she thought, he knows something has changed and she slowly raised her hand to acknowledge his presence.

She could see he hadn't expected that, he assumed she would do what she always did, pulling the curtains closed quickly to sit, with her heart beating loudly in her chest, frightened and alone.

At that moment it was as if she took back control watching as he turned roughly away.

Perhaps, the tables had finally turned as she played him at his own game. Perhaps, there was a power to be had here, a power that could be used to turn his evil into her good.

It was a satisfying thought and for the first time in a long time, she slept deeply and without dreams.

CHAPTER SIXTEEN

It was the first time I'd ever played with Laura other than in practice. The orchestra compositions had been reviewed and like giggling schoolgirls, we were heading off to our first practice session for the new assembly.

'That's Sally isn't it, up ahead?' Laura pointed to the figure walking in the same direction.

Shielding my eyes against the sun, I squinted and looked. 'I think it is.' Cupping a hand to my mouth I called. 'Sal, Sal.' The figure stopped, turned around and waved.

'Are you in this practice session too?' I puffed when we finally caught up with her.

Sally nodded. 'It was a last-minute change, Pauline's sick and they decided to swap us over while she recovers as the other orchestra doesn't start rehearsals until next week. So here I am.' She smiled. 'It's good to see you both, we've been missing each other for weeks now, the schedule is punishing.'

'It gets easier, the longer you're here, honest.' Laura said. 'Next year you'll start losing lectures as the professional performance stuff kicks in.'

Entering the university auditorium never failed to give me a thrill. A magnificent piece of modernist architecture with perfect acoustics ensured everyone, even those in the cheap seats behind the pillars, heard as clearly as those up front and centre.

We were practicing for the annual university music festival and the theme was classical highlights. Today we were going to start on Bolero.

I watched as Sal raised her flute to her mouth waiting for the conductor's instruction. He nodded and the drumbeat began behind her. Counting in she blew the first sweet notes, listening to our plucked strings helped her keep tempo.

We played the entire piece through once before beginning again, this time breaking down the individual instrumental sections needing work.

Two hours later, dripping and exhausted I suggested we all needed coffee.

Nodding mutely, Laura and Sally both agreed.

We dragged ourselves out of the building and across campus to our favourite haunt. It was busy. 'Are these seats taken?' I asked sat on her own at a table for four.

She looked up from her book. 'Of course, please join me.' She had the widest smile.

'Marianne isn't it?' Laura had recognised her.

The girl looked a bit confused but nodded.

'You probably won't remember me, but we played together in my first year. I think you were a couple of years ahead?' Laura smiled. 'You were fab, it still gives me goosebumps when I think about that concert when you played the Little Suite.'

Marianne smiled. 'Thanks, it's nice to be appreciated.' Laughing she asked, 'Do you want an autograph?'

We all giggled, and the ice was broken.

'So, are you musicians too?' Marianne directed the question at me and Sal.

We nodded, 'I'm violin, Sal's flute, and Laura's cello.'

'Yeah, I think I remember you now, didn't you have a moment in a concert recently when you stumbled?'

Laura blushed. 'Goodness, I didn't think anyone had noticed; even the conductor didn't say anything.'

Marianne smiled. 'Apparently, I have a good ear for all the instruments, so they say.' She paused. 'So what brings you all here today?'

'We've just finished the first rehearsal for this year's music festival, and we're shattered. Bolero.' Laura raised her eyes as if that was all that needed saying.

Marianne groaned. 'Oh, I remember Bolero alright, all that precision. It was stressful trying to make sure you kept to time, knowing that others couldn't come in unless you were right there, on the button, when you needed to be. It's one of the Dean's favourites apparently, ever since that ice dance couple …' She paused again .. 'Since the Olympics'

We all nodded in agreement.

'Although I love the piece to listen to, I can't say it's one of my favourites to play.' Sally said.

We looked at her and she flashed right back with. 'It's OK for you two, all you have to do is play along with everyone else, I'm the one in the firing line, starting the whole bloody thing off ..' She stopped '.. Well after Pete and his drum of course.' She shrugged.

I patted her hand. 'Don't get so defensive, we've all been there, remember. You'll be fine. And you were great today. Pity the poor strings who got the biggest criticism.'

I looked at Laura who had the grace to look sheepish.

'We were pretty bad weren't we!' I laughed too.

'Speak for yourself missy, I thought I was practically perfect thank you very much, I think it was the violin section who let the side down.' Laura flung her head back haughtily and then laughed.

'Yep, you're right, we were all pretty poor by comparison to you Sal. It sounded like you'd done plenty of practice.' Laura was gracious in her praise and Sally blushed furiously.

'It's one of my foibles.' Sally shrugged off the compliments.

'So, what are you doing now then Marianne?' I asked.

'Well, as it happens, I've been invited back as this year's invited soloist. I'm very excited.' Marianne clapped her hands and smiled broadly.

Murmurings of 'that's fab' and 'brilliant' came from my friends too, knowing we'd just met a 'celebrity'.

'Wow, what an honour, you must be so pleased. But I thought it was always old people who were asked back, not recent graduates.' I was curious about the policy change.

'So did I. When the call came in, I didn't believe them, thought it was a practical joke until my old tutor called to congratulate me. Turns out the head of school had heard me play in London recently and thought it might be nice to reverse the trend this year, so here I am.' She held her hands out and waved them around the room, mock-bowing to the other coffee lovers.

Looking at her watch she gave a little cry. 'Bugger, I'll be late for my first rehearsal if I don't get a wriggle on.'

Getting up from the seat. 'It's nice to meet you again Laura and I'll look forward to seeing you all in rehearsals.' And slid out of the door.

'Wow, my first meeting with a celebrity musician.' Laura breathed out what we were all thinking.

'She's nice isn't she.' Sal said, and Laura and I nodded in agreement.

The next few weeks passed in a haze of rehearsals and practice alongside the academic rigours to which we were also subjected. It was a punishing timetable and we found ourselves meeting more and more regularly for coffee to talk about anything other than music.

The topic had drifted to the boys we were dating when I noticed Sally was curiously quiet.

'You're a bit quiet there young Sal.' I realised I'd never heard Sally mention seeing anyone at all during the months we'd been friends at uni.

She looked away. 'Well, you're both talking about blokes and things, and I haven't got anything to add'.

I wasn't put off so easily. 'Have you got a boyfriend at home then?'

Sally shook her head.

'Who are you seeing tonight then Jen? The lovely Johann is it this time?'

I shook my head. 'Nope, that's all over. I'm having a bit of a break for a while; you know getting things clear in my head until the festival's out of the way.'

Laura feigned mock surprise, throwing her hand to her head. 'Mon Dieu, ze girl ez not 'aving sex', she exclaimed in an awful attempt at a French accent.

I could feel her looking at me as tears pricked at the side of my eyes.

Putting a hand out she patted me on the arm. 'Are you OK Jen?'

Brushing the tears away roughly. 'Yeah, I'm OK.' I looked at Sal. 'I miss Jamie.'

Sally reached out and grabbed my other hand. 'Why don't you tell him that then? I know he misses you too.'

'It's complicated.' I groaned.

'It can't be that complicated.' Said Sally.

'Oh, you have no idea just how complicated it could be.' Laura confirmed.

Sally looked from one to the other. 'I can't? Are you sure about that?'

I looked at her carefully, she seemed older than her nineteen years as she carried on.

'I guess it's OK to tell you. I'm sure you'll find out anyway soon enough.' And so I told her the bare bones of my relationship with Mr Smithson.

Sally listened open-mouthed and when I finished was quiet.

'Say something, Sal.' I demanded. 'Make me feel a bit better about the whole thing, please.'

I desperately needed her to be OK with me, not find it repulsive as Jamie had.

Sally opened her mouth and then closed it again. 'What did you say his name was Jen?'

'Mr Smithson, Hugh Smithson really but I never called him Hugh, it didn't seem right calling an adult by their first name.' I was reflective. 'Why?'

Sally put her hand on my arm. 'Do you remember when I first met you here, back at the beginning of the year?' She asked.

'Yes, what's that got to do with anything?'

'I was looking for you to talk to you, but then we got caught up with Laura and everything and the time never seemed quite right after that.'

Sally spoke quickly and caught Laura's eye. 'Sorry Laura, not that meeting you was bad or anything, hope you don't think that.'

Laura flashed her a smile. 'Of course not Sal, how could anyone not like to be around me.' She grinned to show it hadn't wounded.

Sally continued. 'I wanted to talk to you about what happened to me the year I went to St Cecilia's, the day you and Jamie broke up, remember?'

I winced. 'I remember. That was a pretty bad time. I was very low for months afterwards. Jamie tried to talk to me, but I couldn't see him. It was just too painful, so I ignored his calls and eventually, he stopped trying.'

'It may have been me he wanted to talk to you about.' Sally said. 'The day you left, when he took you to the station.' She paused. 'I was raped.'

My mouth dropped open and I could see the same reaction in Laura.

'Oh my god, Sally, what happened?' Laura was the first to speak, going around the other side of the booth to hold her hand.

'I don't remember much about it; the police and my parents say I blacked out for a lot of it. But the thing I do remember, the thing I've never told anyone because I didn't believe it.'

She stopped if she was unsure she should go on. Taking a deep breath, she plunged on. 'I never said his name because it didn't feel right, it felt like a lie, like he was throwing it at me to put me off the scent. His name.' She paused again and looked at me. 'His name was Mr Smithson.'

It was my turn to cry out. 'Mr Smithson, really, Mr Smithson what on earth was doing down in Dorset.'

As I said it a light switched on in my mind. My god, he was taking revenge.

'Oh, Sally. It was all my fault and I'm so sorry. I don't know if you'll ever be able to forgive me.' I was crying.

Sally looked at me. 'It's not your fault stupid, how can you think that? It was him that did it, not you. Although from the sounds of it, he could have been looking for you, he sounds even more dangerous than I thought.'

I stopped crying long enough to feel worried. 'Sally, I had a feeling he was possessive, but it never crossed my mind he might do something when he left the school, I just assumed he'd moved on. It was only when Laura told me what happened to her I started to think differently about what he'd done to me.' I paused. 'That's why Jamie and I split up, he couldn't stand the thought I'd let someone do the things he did to me willingly. That man spoilt me, he spoilt me for any love I might have. That's why I have these casual flings, they don't matter you see, they don't mean anything, so the sex is easy.'

I was all talked out and subsided back into my seat.

Laura could see profound shock was kicking in for both of us and went to the counter. 'Three teas and make them strong with plenty of sugar please?' Handing over the money, she took the mugs back to the table and pushed one in front of each of us.

'Drink.' She ordered.

We both drank and then sat quietly digesting the revelations that had just been shared.

'I never thought I'd hear that name again, you know.' I said. 'I think back now and realise what a fool I was, but I was just a teenager, didn't know any better, didn't think.' I was bitter, it had never occurred to me he might try something even more shocking.

'I haven't had a boyfriend since.' Sally admitted. 'I can't bear the idea of someone pawing at me.'

Laura spoke up. 'Seeing as we're sharing secrets, you'd better know mine too Sal, just for the record and so I'm not left out.' She smiled thinly, trying to make it into a joke, but none of us were laughing.

'The day you first met up with Jenny I wasn't too pleased either Sally.' She held up both hands in apology. 'The guy that did for me was in the audience at a performance. 'She paused. 'Again! I see him most nights standing outside my hall of residence, just watching my room. It gives me the creeps to think there's a pervert out there who knows what I'm doing and when.' Looking away, she apologised to me. 'Sorry, I've never told you that bit before Jen.'

I grabbed her hand it was cool to the touch. 'It's OK Laura, you know that. I don't need to know anything, but you really should go to the police. Standing outside your hall of residence night after night is too much of a coincidence, you should be able to get a restraining order at least.'

Sally piped up. 'He's not Mr Smithson too, is he?'

I smiled bleakly. 'Fortunately not Sal, this one is called Johnson.'

I decided it was wise not to mention the phantasm I'd once seen outside Tom's room.

Three hours later, the police were very polite but, they said, there was nothing they could do if someone was just standing on the public highway. They weren't committing an offence after all. The woman police officer even questioned how she could know it was her he was interested in, he could just be out for a smoke.

But they did promise to drive by and check that night.

Laura did not feel reassured. It seemed as if no one in authority took her seriously.

'Can you stay with me tonight, Jen?' She pleaded. 'I don't want to be on my own and like you, I'm off men at the moment.'

Despite my workload, I agreed. 'But only if we go to bed at a reasonable time, I've got a heavy day tomorrow.'

Laura nodded and smiled, and that night we both checked what was going on outside her window, there was no one there. A police car drove slowly by and then looped around the car park at the back of the science block and back again.

'Do you think he knew I went to the police Jen?' Laura wanted reassurance.

'How could he possibly know Laura? We kept checking behind us all the way there, there was no one following us. Perhaps he just got fed up and decided to do something else instead.' I'm sure I sounded more confident than I felt. Since the coffee shop revelations, I'd had an uncomfortable feeling of being watched and deciphered too.

Putting it down to paranoia brought on by the conversations with Laura, Sally and the police, I tried to dismiss it from my mind, but it did raise the awkward question of where Mr Smithson was now.

Over the years I was sure I'd seen him at regular intervals. In the distance, at a concert or the station. But he was too far away to identify clearly and always appeared somewhat changed, not the man I'd known as a teenager.

Sally's confession had worried me. Was it the same man? And if so, had it been me who had changed him into a monster so vicious he would attack and rape in broad daylight? I fervently hoped it wasn't him, but the coincidences were too many to ignore.

I considered contacting Jamie to tell him what Sally had revealed, but shame stopped me. I didn't want to reopen old wounds, especially as Sally had been adamant no one else knew the name. So I waited sure that the right moment would come, and that when it did, Jamie would help me know what to do.

CHAPTER SEVENTEEN

The end-of-year music festival loomed and all thoughts of men, Mr Smithson, or Johnson amongst them, were put on hold. Wrapped up in the music we were safe from the outside world.

The auditorium became our second home, and we got closer to Marianne as well, pleased and surprised when she sought us out during rehearsal breaks.

'What are you all up to this evening then?' Marianne asked after a particularly intense rehearsal.

'Bar.' Laura and I said at once.

'Bed.' said Sally who looked exhausted, perfecting the Bolero was taking its toll.

'Oh, come on, you can't just go to bed.' I protested. 'You do need some downtime too. Come with us to the bar, you need to have some fun.' I cajoled and put on a bright encouraging smile.

'I'll come if you do.' Offered Marianne

Sally relented. 'Okay as you put it like that then, but one drink for me and home, I'm dead on my feet here.' She wobbled deliberately. 'See'. We all laughed.

The bar was packed as usual and Laura out in front pushed her way through the crowds to grab the last table, pulling stools around and staking her claim.

By the time the rest of us made it she had valiantly fought off several other groups.

'Right then girls, what are you having to drink?' Marianne offered.

'Spritzer for me please.' From Laura.

'I'll have a vodka and coke please.' It was my drink du jour.

Sally asked for a pint of lager shandy. She fended off our comments saying it would be enough to carry her through each of us having several drinks.

When Marianne eventually sat down, we were keen to hear what she had to say about our performances.

'Well.' She started, looking closely at each of us. I felt uncomfortable under her stare sure she was going to pick out every mistake I knew I'd made.

'Well, it's like this see, you're all too bloody good, I'm not surprised each of you has been singled out for solos.'

I looked at my friends, their pleasure at her complement shone across them and I grinned, then felt shy; this was the star of the show and such high praise from someone who wasn't friend or family was an experience I'd rarely had before.

Laura expressed it the best of all. 'Aw shucks.' she drawled. 'That's mighty kind of yer t'say'.

Marianne laughed. 'You really should be in show business you know, with that fake accent you'd go down a storm.' Laura punched her on the arm playfully and then apologised when she realised who she'd hit.

'Come on Laura, you know me well enough now not to worry about something like that.' Marianne admonished.

She looked at us all even more closely. 'Have you decided what you're going to do after uni yet?'

I was the only one with a half-formed plan. 'I'd like to be accepted by one of the big orchestras, you know the Phil perhaps.' I blushed sure they'd all laugh at my dreams.

No-one did. 'You could do that Jenny you know, you've got the talent.' Marianne was diffident in her praise, but it hit the right note and I smiled at her.

'What about you Laura?' she asked.

Laura squirmed. 'Well, I'd quite like to be wherever my best friend is really.'

I put my arm around her gently and smiled.

Sally looked up. 'I've still got a couple of years before I need to make any decisions, but I think it might be nice to be part of a small group, orchestras look like they might be quite lonely places.'

Marianne smiled at her. 'They are, for some; not everyone though, only the special few who see through the ego, pomp and circumstance of it all.'

We looked at her expecting more. It was Laura, again, who asked the question. 'What will you do when the festival is finished?'

'Well.' she said slowly. 'I'm really glad you asked because, like Sally I always feel a bit lost in an orchestra. I'm at my happiest when I'm busking, to be honest, just a small group in Covent Garden or outside a cathedral, you know.' She trailed off.

Her comment reminded me of a past conversation 'You remember we talked ages ago about us playing together?' Laura nodded so I carried on. 'Perhaps, that's what we could do, while we think about what to do next.'

Laura looked at me. 'Like an ensemble?'

I nodded. 'Yes, if Sally and Marianne joined us, it would be fun, at least until we all decide what we want to do next that is.'

I looked at Sally and Marianne. 'What do you think, do you want to give it a go over the summer and see how we get on?'

They both nodded enthusiastically. 'That would be great.' said Sally. 'And I'm sure Mummy and Daddy would have us down in Dorset while we sorted out a repertoire, what do you think?'

Marianne looked doubtful. 'But they don't know me.'

Sally and I both laughed. 'You don't know them, they'd love it, honestly.' Said Sally.

Laura looked at me curiously. 'Are you sure that's a wise idea, Jamie and all?'

Sally broke in saying. 'It's okay, Jamie's working away, he won't be around for a while.'

Any hopes I'd had were doused. 'Oh', that's a shame, it would have been good to see him.'

'Jamie?' Queried Marianne

'My ex-boyfriend and Sal's brother.' I explained.

'Ah, I see.' Said Marianne, even though she didn't see it at all.

The festival began in the usual way. A rag week parade through the streets in aid of charity and the musicians doing their best imitation of several brass bands with wind and string added on the side.

Over the week there would be concerts large and small, master classes and solo performances of every musical genre. In between performances, students busked in the shopping parade and gave free performances in local churches and halls, all in aid of charity.

The highlight would be Saturday night's orchestral extravaganza where both orchestras came together in one huge performance. Before that though, they vied with each other to see who could draw the biggest audiences and give the most rousing performances.

When it came to Bolero, the rivalry was at its peak, each orchestra had prepared a version of Ravel's score to be performed on different nights, the audience had a scoring system and boxes had been placed strategically by the exits to capture the voting slips.

Sally was nervous. This was the first time she had played in front of such a large audience alone. Even being part of a large orchestra was no consolation, she would set the tone for the rest of the team.

Standing in the wings peering out as the auditorium filled, she was bemused when one of the concert volunteers handed her a box saying. 'A bloke left this for you Sally.'

She opened it and inside was a perfect single yellow rose with a label hand tied to it, The sweetest one'. Looking around she tried to see if someone was playing a joke but couldn't see anything. She hurried back to the practice room. When the others saw her coming, they all held up the same boxes.

'You got one too Sal?' I asked the obvious question.

'Apparently.' She agreed.

'What did the note say?' Sally opened the box and showed them.

Silently, we showed her ours.

Red, pink, and black roses nestled in cream paper-lined boxes, each with a handwritten tag and a different sentiment.

My beautiful girl read Marianne's; Laura's said My perfect rose and on mine was written, My beloved.

'Is someone playing a practical joke on us?' Said Laura in a loud voice. 'If so, they can stop now because I don't think it's funny'.

We looked around at our fellow musicians who all held up their hands in denial and shook their heads.

I spoke first. 'Well, whatever it's all about we need to forget it for the time being, we've got a job to do, and this can wait until later.' I put my box on the nearest table.

The others agreed and as one put their gifts on the table with mine to be collected after the concert.

Laura looked out over the audience and spotted him immediately, it was as if an inner missile had latched on to him. She reached her foot over and poked me in the foot.

Looking up, I hissed. 'What did you do that for?'

'He's here, middle right about twelve rows back.' Hissed Laura back.

I looked to where Laura was pointing and strained to see the man who had been trailing Laura.

A man lifted his hand and waved slightly, and my heart lurched, Mr Smithson.

He smiled and I felt bile rise in my mouth, swallowing it down I wiped sweaty palms on my dress and looked again. He was looking directly at me with a smile that said 'gotcha'.

I was half out of my seat when the orchestra rose to welcome the conductor on stage. He seated us and lifted his baton, assuming we were all ready to play. He looked at me, as first violin it was my job to lead the rest of the orchestra. Feeling disconnected but knowing there was nothing else I could do I nodded and raised my violin indicating I was ready even though I had never felt less ready for anything in my life.

The conductor swept the baton down and we began to play.

CHAPTER EIGHTEEN

We gathered in the wings immediately after the performance, each flying in from our position on the stage.

I had kept beat with the conductor at the same time as trying to keep sight of Mr Smithson in the audience. At a crucial moment in the repertoire, when it had my fullest attention, he must have left. I didn't see him leave, but strangely Marianne did.

Looking at us she spoke quietly. 'There was a man in the audience tonight, one who's haunted my dreams for years. One I didn't think I'd see ever again.'

We all looked at her, it was as if we knew what she was going to say.

Suddenly she fainted. Collapsing against one of the flaps like an opera singer.

People rushed up from all sides, water was brought, and someone even fished out a small bottle of smelling salts.

Sitting up, Marianne looked pale and drawn. 'Can we go and find somewhere quiet to talk please?' She asked.

We all nodded and helped her back to the practice room. We'd all been invited to a communal late supper with our various parents and a large table had been booked at a local hotel so taking charge, I went out to meet them in the bar.

I was surprised to see Jamie with them, that hadn't been part of the plan. I felt myself frowning at him even though he smiled broadly back.

'You were all marvellous.' He was enthusiastic and grasped my hands firmly.

The touch of him sent a tingle down my spine and I shivered. 'Are you cold?' His concern was genuine, and it touched me deeply.

'No, not really.' I shook my head and paused before looking at him closely. 'It's so good to see you, Jamie'.

He nodded back. 'And you Jenny'. Dropping one hand he led me back to the parental group who were also enthusiastically praising the night's performance.

I looked at them, focusing on my father. 'Something's come up, can we meet you at the restaurant instead of going for a drink first and we may bring a friend along, if that's OK with you?'

My mother was clearly bothered. 'What's wrong darling? Are you alright? Is there anything we can do?'

I shook my head. 'No, I don't think so, at least not yet, maybe later, possibly.' I held out my hands to them hoping they'd understand. 'Give us forty-five minutes and we'll see you there'.

I turned back to Jamie. 'You'll be there, won't you? I'll see you later?'

Jamie nodded, his face full of concern. 'Of course, I wouldn't miss it'.

I headed back to the practice room to find Marianne alone. 'Where are the others?'

'They've gone for a quick post-performance debrief with the head of music. They won't be long.'

I sat down and grasped her hand and looked into her eyes. 'The man, the one you saw, where was he sitting?' I asked it quietly, fearing the answer.

'Oh, I don't know, roughly in the middle somewhere.' Marianne pointed vaguely out to the right with her hand. 'I only noticed him when he got up to leave.' She paused. 'He looked right at me, it felt like he could see right into my soul'.

I went cold, it was in the same area Mr Smithson had been sitting in. 'Did this man..' I paused, not wanting to ask the question I knew I must. I took a deep breath, '..did he have a name? Do you know his name?'

Marianne looked at me curiously. 'Of course I do it was my old music teacher, Hugh Smithson.'

The bottom dropped out of my world.

'What did he do?' I whispered even though I already knew the answer, my heart was drumming so hard I was sure the world would hear it.

'He raped me.' Marianne said simply. 'And then he told the head I had provoked him, led him on.'

I clung to her hand even harder. I was drowning, struggling for air, wanting the unfolding nightmare to end. My breath rasped and I gasped, pulling oxygen into my lungs, feeling faint but knowing I needed to hold it all together.

'Are you ok Jenny, you look very pale?' It was Marianne's turn to be concerned.

'I will be. Let's wait till the others get here and I'll tell you more.' Glancing over my shoulder at the four rose boxes that still lay on the side table it was obvious who had sent them, but the question was why.

We sat in silence holding hands for what felt like hours but was probably just a few minutes until the others came to rescue us.

Sally noticed immediately. 'Now what's going on? You both look like you've seen a ghost.'

My smile felt feeble. 'We have, metaphorically speaking and I'm surprised you didn't see him too, the rest of us did.'

Sally looked confused. 'See who?' And then looking at our faces realised we weren't talking about something pleasant. Her hand flew to her mouth, 'No .. it can't be him.' She sat down heavily.

Laura and I looked at each other nodding, I was the first to speak. 'It seems Laura's Mr Johnson and our Mr Smithson are the same person'.

Marianne looked shocked. 'You know him?'

I was grim. 'We all know him, in our own way. It seems he has a thing for young female musicians.' I waved my hand at the table. 'And I'll bet anything you like those are from him'.

We all looked at the boxes. Sally stood up. 'I'm going to be sick.' And she fled for the bathroom.

Laura and Marianne both started talking at once, so I put my hands up to quiet them.

'Look, Marianne Laura, Sally and I are all supposed to be having a late supper with our parents, I've already put them off a little, but we need to go otherwise they'll worry and wonder what's going on. I mentioned we might bring a friend and right now I think you need to come with us too, I don't want anyone to be on their own tonight, it doesn't feel safe.' I hoped my look was stern enough to counter any arguments.

Fortunately, Marianne agreed. 'I'd like that, the thought of going back to my hotel room alone fills me with dread, but I still don't know how you all know him.'

I held my hand up again. 'Tomorrow I think, not tonight. It's too raw tonight and we've all had a shock. Tomorrow we can talk and decide what to do.' Picking up the four boxes I stuffed them in the large bin. 'But I do know we need to get rid of these.' My face was grim as I pushed them down firmly before slamming the lid on.

Sally returned to the practice room and fell into Laura's open arms. 'Marianne's coming out to supper with us all tonight and we've agreed we'll get together tomorrow to decide what to do. Is that alright with you?'

Nodding mutely Sally picked up her flute case and added it to the other instruments in the locker room.

Supper passed uneventfully and we all relaxed in the company of our families. If any of our parents noticed anything no one said. Slowly the volume increased as conversations struggled to be heard over others chattering.

Marianne was an instant hit with everyone especially when my father pinned her down to ask her about potential careers for all three darling daughters.

Jamie had kept a place next to him for me and I was grateful for his attention.

'You look tired Jen.' It was a statement rather than a question.

'I am rather Jamie; it's been a rough few weeks and this is just the start of it.' I heard the subtext in my words, the festival would be easy by comparison to tomorrow's discussion.

I smiled thinly. 'How are you anyway, I only ever get your news third-hand from Sal these days.'

'Busy.' He admitted. 'But good, working for a car company has its perks, designing for them is even better and I've been doing some testing on an engine I worked on in Bahrain'.

I laughed. 'Bahrain' isn't that a dry county? How on earth do you manage without the daily pint?'

'It's not as bad as you think you know.' The foreign compounds are effectively independent of those particular rules, you just have to be careful and respectful, that's all.'

I dug him in the ribs. 'Get you, with your fancy jet set lifestyle'.

He slapped my hand playfully. 'And what about you? I can see a star rising on the horizon and it has your name on it.' He swung his arm in an arc to emphasise the point.

'Do you think so?' I was curious to know what he thought of my performance.

'Yep, I really do, all four of you, Marianne included, just have something ..' he struggled to finish the sentence, 'something extra, you know?'

'I can see it in Laura and of course Sal, wasn't the Bolero amazing? She's just so good; and I can see it in Marianne of course, being asked back to be the university soloist is an honour and is only extended to the best musicians.' I looked down at the table. 'But me, well I hear me all the time and I know it feels good, I assume everyone is the same.'

My father sat to my right caught my words. 'I know I am biased darling, but even so, I couldn't be more proud of you than I already am. You are young, beautiful and have a wonderful talent. Enjoy it all, you deserve it, the hard work you've put in can't be claimed by many.' He patted me on the arm and turned back to talk to Miriam and Marianne.

I blushed. 'Thanks Dad I love you too.' and kissed him on the back of his neck.

I turned back to Jamie. 'I wanted to get in touch a while ago but didn't know how to start the conversation, and then you were out of the country so I couldn't.' I looked across at Sal and glanced back at him.

He caught the look. 'Is everything ok Jenny, I mean really?' His face flashed concern again.

I shook my head, saying quietly. 'No not really.'

A look I couldn't fathom flashed across his face. 'Is it Sal, has something happened?'

I nodded. 'And with me, and Laura and Marianne in fact.' Looking down, I tried to make my mind up about what to do next. 'Look, are you staying for a couple of days?'

He looked surprised. 'I wasn't planning to but if you need me then, of course, I will, I can make my excuses to Ma and Pa. They won't mind if I'm back home a day or two late and I'm due some leave from work.'

I nodded gratefully. 'It would be great if you could. Where are you staying, I'll come and collect you tomorrow. I don't know what time it will be, and you could be hanging around, would that be alright?'

He smiled. 'Don't worry, I'm sure I can find something to read while I'm waiting and if I'm not there just leave a note at reception for me to meet you somewhere. And we're all at the same hotel; your parents, mine, and Laura's. Just one big happy family.' He laughed.

Sally watched our conversation from the other end of the table and turning to Laura she said. 'It looks like those two might just be getting along again.'

Laura looked and nudged Marianne. 'That's the famous Jamie.'

Marianne nodded. 'I guessed as much.'

It was long past midnight when the party broke up with cries of 'goodnight darling', 'see you tomorrow' and 'you were all marvellous.'

The families walked the short distance to their hotel and we walked Marianne back to hers before heading back to our respective halls.

Dropping Sally off first, Laura slipped her arm through mine and slowed her pace.

'I can't believe Mr Johnson and your Mr Smithson are one and the same. But it makes a creepy sort of sense when you think about it.'

I nodded. 'I didn't tell you that I saw Mr Smithson outside my room one night. To be honest I haven't looked since but I'm sure he's out there. To be honest I don't want to know. In my room, I feel cosy and safe. Out here, I feel alone and vulnerable; except when I'm with you of course.' I added hastily.

'Can I stay with you tonight, Jenny?' Laura asked, 'I don't want to be in my place after everything that's happened today and now I know he's not who he says he is I'm really frightened.'

I squeezed her arm. 'Of course you can Lau. I was going to suggest it anyway. It's what friends are for. I'm not sure I want to be alone either. It would be good to have some company for a change.'

Back in my room, I pulled out the roller bed for Laura. Adding sheets and a duvet I donated one of my pillows and hauled her some pyjamas.

We cleaned our teeth companionably at the sink. 'Look at us, we could be an old married couple.' I gurned showing her a mouthful of FreshDent toothpaste.

Tucked up in bed, Laura sighed. 'Part of me wants to look out of the window.'

'Don't go there Laura.' I instructed sleepily. 'It's much too late for anyone to be out and anyway, I need to rest.'

Laura lay wakeful listening to Jenny's gentle snores, wondering if she should risk a look and eventually, quietly raised the edge of one curtain and peeked out. There was no one there. She heaved a sigh of relief, climbed back into bed and fell asleep.

CHAPTER NINETEEN

Marianne headed down the hall to the practice room, her sanctuary away from the everyday stresses of living in London.

She was on her third practice piece when he stuck his head around the door. 'Marianne?'

'Yes.' She replied without stopping.

'Hello, I'm Mr Smithson. I've been asked to come and accompany you for some pieces you're working on.' He stretched out his hand and she took it gingerly, teachers didn't normally shake the hand of their pupils.

She wondered what had happened to Tilly, the music assistant who normally accompanied her.

'Tilly got called away and asked me to pop in.' He said it as if he was reading her thoughts. 'She said you wouldn't mind.'

Marianne wasn't sure if she minded or not but decided to go along with it.

'OK. These are the pieces I'm working on right now, are you familiar with them Mr Smithson?'

He took them from her and looked them over. 'Well, I know the Telemann Concerto quite well and I've often played the Brahms so why don't we start with those and take it from there.'

Taking the sheets off him she placed them on the stand, raised the viola and bow and looked at him. 'Ok, let's start with the Brahms then as that's the one I think needs most work.'

They played for about twenty minutes, stopping every so often to talk about emphasis and phrasing, trying out different variations and revisiting refrains she thought perfected, but now realised could be improved, sometimes dramatically.

When they stopped for a break, she was sweaty and her breathing was laboured, she'd certainly had a workout.

Brushing the hair out of her eyes she caught him watching her.

'Would you like a coffee after practice?' He was guileless in the asking.

She considered his question carefully; it was something she frequently did with friends after school had finished for the day. Now that she was in the sixth form, they didn't have the same forced prep periods before supper as the younger years did. They could in theory, or so their teachers told them, be trusted to get on with prep in their own time. It was however unheard of for a teacher to take a pupil for coffee.

'I don't think so Mr Smithson, it would hardly be appropriate would it.' She looked at him archly, daring him to contradict her.

'There's nothing sinister about my invitation. It's just that sometimes it can help to talk about the music as well as play it. Sometimes, discussion can help you understand more than the notes are telling you, but it's up to you.' He shrugged diffidently as if the case were closed.

She reconsidered. 'OK then, let's go now, that way I'll be able to put our discussion into practice when I get back.'

Picking up her coat and case she walked to the door, turning back to see if he was following her.

Wetherby School was in the centre of town. It was handy for boarders and day pupils alike and they often congregated in one or two cafes where they were well known. Some of the older ones whose parents were overseas were known to work in the cafes during the summer months, for something to do rather than the meagre wages they paid out.

He chose a booth at the back of Jacks Café and Marianne was grateful. It was bad enough walking through the café with a teacher in tow, she didn't want any more gossip than could already be helped. She could almost feel the others sniggering behind her as she sat down. No doubt they'd be on at her when she got back.

Mr Smithson ordered two coffees', one black for him, and one white for her.

She cupped her hands around the mug and looked at him. 'So, what does the music say to you, Mr Smithson?' She couldn't have been ruder had she tried, but he didn't seem to notice.

'You're a sassy one aren't you Marianne? I wonder if any other teachers have ever said that to you?' He was mild in his rebuke.

She laughed. 'All the time Mr Smithson, all the time.'

'Music.' He looked skyward as if contemplating the majesty of it. 'Is something you feel, not something you just listen to it. The greatest of musicians knew this instinctively, others need to be taught it.' He looked at her. 'Do you know it, Marianne?'

She wasn't quite sure how to reply and shrugged it off. 'Not really Mr Smithson. I like playing and I like listening equally, but I can't say either makes me feel much of anything at all.' She neglected to inform him that she didn't just feel the music, she was the music.

He looked at her carefully, weighing up what she'd just said and she had the odd impression of being weighed in Anubis's balance scale. 'I understand from Tilly that you're hoping to make it to music college when you finish your A levels?'

She was rather unsettled to learn she had been discussed in this way but supposed it must be the normal course of teacherly conversations. 'Well, yes, I hope so.'

'If you can't feel the music then you won't get in.' He said it as a matter of fact that was not up for discussion. 'If you like, I can help you get to the level you need to be. Would you like me to help you do that Marianne?'

In later years, she would often reflect on what it was that made her say yes.

Their next practice fell on a Thursday afternoon. The school was quiet, it often was on a Thursday as most pupils were out on the playing fields being forced around a hockey pitch or tennis courts by the unrelenting games mistresses.

They continued to work on the viola pieces she was preparing, stopping to discuss the finer points of notation and emphasis.

She didn't like the way he manhandled her sometimes to get her into what he thought was the right position, but she put up with it because it almost always worked out better than before.

His hands were sweaty, and his breath was stale with tobacco and coffee. But he did have a torso she enjoyed watching covertly and Marianne found herself warming to him, despite her misgivings. Regularly, they would have coffee at the back of the café, it became so frequent that even the other girls stopped taunting her about it. Instead, they just asked what they were talking about. Music she would reply, and they would laugh, as if they didn't believe her.

When his hands fell on her leg, accidentally on purpose she was sure, she moved swiftly out of the way.

He apologised immediately. 'Sorry about that Marianne, my mistake.'

Mistake, how could it be a mistake? She was confused and it showed on her face.

'My hand just sort of fell, sorry, it does that sometimes, I have a bit of muscle weakness, that's all.' He held up his hand as if to peel back the skin and show her the weak muscles.

'That's OK.' Although it wasn't really.

Thursdays became 'their day' for practice and coffee. Although she still didn't fully trust him, she did like him. He was an amusing companion and he never failed to draw out some extra expression from the music that she hadn't realised was there.

Because she was improving so quickly, she started to overlook his little faults. The trick of his 'weak hand' that seemed to know just when to fall conveniently on her breasts when he was adjusting the instrument in her hands.

He always apologised profusely, holding up the hand in evidence, but she was wise to him and chose not to say anything about it after all, it was just a brush here and there, she thought, and sometimes when her nipples became hard because of it, she would admit silently to herself that she even quite liked it, just a little.

The Christmas concerts had come and gone, and they were now practising for grade eight exams. All the pre-prepared pieces were fine, but Marianne was having problems sight reading and this took up most of their time. The practice sheets were discarded in favour of random pieces from a variety of sources, jazz, rock and roll, and the blues. None were intended for the viola specifically, but they did allow her to find a different way of expressing herself.

After a particularly thrilling encounter with Jazz, she was high on adrenaline when he made his move.

Marianne was bent over her viola case putting the instrument away when she heard the door click. She assumed Mr Smithson had left the room and half turned to find him right behind her.

He held out his hand and she took it without thinking and he walked her over to the desk.

'Take off your panties.' He ordered.

'What?' She couldn't believe what she'd just heard.

He repeated the instruction. 'Take off your knickers, if you don't I'll take them off for you.' His voice was firm, and his eyes glittered with a coldness she hadn't seen before.

'What on earth do you mean, I'm not taking off my knickers for you or anyone else, get off me you old letch.' She pushed him away and turned to grab her case and music. She knew she'd been right not to trust him.

He grabbed her arm and pulled her back to the side of the desk, pushing her roughly down on top of it. 'I told you if you didn't take them off, I'd take them off for you, but you didn't do as I asked did you? In fact, you weren't very nice at all.' He spat the words at her and she realised he meant every word of it.

A scream was building in her throat.

He laughed. 'Go on scream, it's a practice room and no one will hear, they're too well insulated, you know that.'

She let one rip anyway just in case someone happened to be right outside the door, knowing all the time how unlikely it was because it was Thursday, and the whole school was enjoying the sunshine outside on a Thursday.

He slapped her hard across the face. 'Scream again and I'll tape your mouth up and you wouldn't want that would you?'

She shook her head mutely, her face stinging from the slap.

'Now, take your panties off, you know you want to.' He ordered again.

She complied.

He took her from behind, bent over the desk as if she were being whipped and that was how she felt. Hot, salty tears streamed down her face as he slammed into her, harder and harder. The pain was unbelievable, she thought she would die from the hurt of it. Finally, he pushed in one last time and she felt a hot gushing flowing up inside her. He pulled out of her roughly and turned her over. Hungrily he pushed up her blouse and pulled her bra aside. His mouth was on her breasts, and she felt her villainous nipples responding to his tongue, she couldn't contain the moan of pleasure as his fingers played with her clitoris and when he brought her to orgasm it was a hot mixture of pleasure and shame that coursed through her body. How could it have let her down like that, it was a question she'd be asking for the rest of her life.

'Now that wasn't so bad was it, Marianne?' He looked satisfied

She couldn't answer him and turned away.

He slapped her again. 'Answer me, Marianne, tell me that was good, tell me you enjoyed it.' He demanded.

'It was good, and I enjoyed it, Mr Smithson.' Her voice was small. 'Can I go now please?' her eyes pleaded with him and he, the victor, nodded. He unlocked the door while she retrieved her knickers and slid out.

Back in her room, the tears flowed afresh. She didn't understand what had just happened, she didn't know why her body had let her down or how she had let herself be defiled in such a way. She intuited, rightly, that her life had changed, she had grown up and knew the world to be a darker place than she had thought.

She washed carefully, it was painful washing between her legs and his stuff kept coming out of her. Putting a sanitary towel in her knickers she lay down on the bed and wept.

Eventually, she must have slept because the light had gone from the sky when she opened her eyes. Thinking over the events of earlier Marianne realised she had to tell someone what had happened and got up, wincing with the pain in her upper legs and abdomen.

Knocking on the headmaster's door, she was summoned inside.

'Ah, Marianne, just the person I wanted to speak to. Sit down.' He indicated a seat opposite his desk.

'I've just had a conversation with Mr Smithson who tells me that you've become a little bit too clingy, and you made advances to him today which he had to rebuff, is this true?'

Marianne could hardly believe what he was saying, that wasn't what had happened, was it? It was him who had assaulted her, but then the memory of her body's response to his touch flooded back her cheeks blushed.

She shook her head. 'That's not what happened at all, he forced himself on me and did things I didn't want to do and ..' She couldn't continue and started to cry.

The Head, never good with crying girls tried unsuccessfully to comfort her.

'There, there, I'm sure it was all just a misunderstanding between you. We all know how emotional you young girls can get when there's an attractive man around don't we? I'm sure everything will be alright.' His dismissal of her statement shocked her to the core, and she stared at him.

'It was not a misunderstanding, and I'm not emotional because of some silly schoolgirl crush, he attacked me and locked the door so I couldn't leave and I screamed but no one could hear because we were in the music rooms.'

'That's not what Mr Smithson said my dear.'

The Head was patronising. After all, he had four decades experience of the emotional unsteadiness of young girls and how they could read a sandwich into a picnic basket if they wanted to.

'He told me you positively jumped on him, and he said he was worried he'd given you the wrong impression by taking you for a coffee after practice.'

He looked at her knowingly. 'We did know you have been having coffee regularly, so you must see how it looks, Marianne?' There was a finality to his words as if he was going so far and no further.

Unfortunately, she did see how it looked. She realised a trap had been set and she had walked straight into it. You could almost say she'd been led to this very conversation by the nose all along, like a prize-winning heifer at the County Show. The coffee, she was coming to understand had all been part of an elaborate game plan that had her at the centre of the trap he had sprung.

'I'd like to talk to the police.' She made the statement firmly; she didn't want to be dismissed.

'Oh, I don't think there's any need for all that nonsense, now is there Marianne? Mr Smithson has already resigned, he said he thought it would be in everyone's best interests if he left immediately. He doesn't want a stain hanging over the school and neither do we, do we, Marianne?' He stared her down. 'After all, what are they going to make of it all, a young girl leading a teacher on and then crying wolf, come now, you know that wouldn't end well, don't you?'

Turning back his back on her he threw out. 'I think that's all for now. If you have any other problems, next time talk to Matron about them first, please. I know that young girls your age are often out with boys these days, but we don't want it getting out of hand now do we?' She was dismissed.

Getting up painfully from the chair, she backed out of the room vowing never to trust any man again.

Three days later the pain began in earnest, it was hot and lancing and struck to the very heart of her. Matron put it down to a stomach bug, but she knew better. It was Mr Smithson coming back to haunt her.

CHAPTER TWENTY

Leaning against the lamppost, collar turned up against the wind and hat pulled down low, over his brow, Mr Smithson fancied he looked like some old-time detective from the 1950's and hunkered further down in his overcoat.

He could see her through the curtains, a black silhouette against the harsh light. Stretching her arms up to take off her jumper, reaching round her back to undo the bra. Bending over to slip off jeans and then panties. In his mind he could feel the touch of her, of doing those things he knew she loved and slowly, turning her around to face him so he could look deep into her soul and know she still loved him.

'Jenny.' He whispered the name, a caress across his voice box.

Mr Smithson, was there, outside under the streetlight most nights. He knew Jenny's routine almost better than she did for we all do things unconsciously, without thinking. The way we brush our hair, clean our teeth, the route we take to work or lectures and the times we habitually rise and go to bed.

He also knew how she was with the lovers who had crossed her path, knowing instinctively the way she would be with them, how she would teach them what she liked, what she wanted.

At first, he had been angry beyond belief. Taking his rage out on girls he came across, indiscriminately, without thought or planning. It had been a dangerous time for him, and he had fought hard to bring himself under control; it would not do, it would not do at all to be caught at this stage in the game.

That first summer, after he left Jamieson's, he had travelled to France. Jenny's parents had been most helpful in sharing the details of their villa when they had been friendly and he located it without difficulty. Asking the locals in the village, they pointed him to the English Quarter as they called it; all he had to do was watch and wait to see who went where and with whom.

Hugh could remember it now, the tight feeling in his chest and the pain in his palms as his nails dug in, seeing her for the first time with a boy, a boy she was clearly in love with.

How dare she, how dare she dismiss him from her life without a second thought. He was incandescent and almost let his presence be known. By breathing slowly, deeply, he was able to bring his heart rate down and become calmer.

He watched both houses for a few days, noting the comings and goings and who seemed to belong where. Careful conversation with villagers in the local bar helped him establish the names and details of the family he didn't yet know, filing the details away in the repository marked 'revenge'.

When he intuited it was becoming apparent that he wasn't really on holiday, that he was snooping around, he left.

Jenny's light flicked off.

Time to go he thought, and he turned away for his second stop of the evening.

Laura always knew when he arrived. She looked out for him every night and he took a vicious pleasure in her reaction to his presence. Closing the curtains, she assumed it kept him out of her room, the reality was thin curtains, coupled with bright lights, put her even more deliciously to the forefront of his mental stage so much so that this was where he stayed, long after she had turned the lights out and climbed into bed.

While he watched the window he regularly thought about 'his girls', as he considered them. These were the special ones, those who meant more than any others and it was a stroke of luck they had all ended up at the same university.

They were all beautiful in their own way. Classic good looks that showed their breeding, long hair in an infinite variety of colours; no one could ever accuse him of having prejudices when it came to the female form. Voluptuous and curvy, straight and narrow hipped; they were all the same to him; what mattered was the passion in their soul. Passion that most frequently manifested in a rare musical ability.

Of the four, Laura was the only one who saw him. There had been a couple of times he had almost been caught out by Jenny. London and then ... he struggled to remember .. ah, yes, that was it. Marianne's performance. But apart from that, he'd remained hidden, on the sidelines, watching and waiting for the right moment to reveal himself.

Marianne. He rolled the name around his mouth and head. It had an exotic ring to it he found provocative and inviting. She was his beautiful girl, stunning with model good looks and the dark sloe eyes of the Mediterranean. When she had refused him, he knew it was a come-on. So many girls these days said No, when they meant yes, and she had been a classic.

Her earnest glances over coffee had convinced him she idolised him. After all, every other girl at Wetherby was trying to get into his trousers, why wouldn't she?

He had known from an early age, the effect his looks had on girls and women alike. As a teenager, he was amused by the amount of attention lavished on him by the school's cohort of girls right through to the oldest teachers. He worked his way through them all, finding those he liked the most were the teenagers, right on the cusp of adulthood. Older than his friends, despite being the same age, they had a knowingness and confidence that was ripe for cultivation.

Ageing allowed him to grow into his looks, using his movie star charisma to its greatest effect. Regular weights sessions kept his muscles sculpted and running kept his body toned; the time spent outdoors, coaching the hockey, tennis and lacrosse teams ensured he always had a healthy tan as well as keeping an eye on the girls he coveted; ensuring they were healthy and happy was, he felt, a key part of his role in their life.

He'd even tried out prostitutes, the younger the better. Holidays from work were spent trawling the neighbourhoods not usually found on the pages of guidebooks, picking up one or two every night for quick and easy blow jobs or fucks in the back of his car. It was sexually satisfying, but held no romance, no thrill, no emotion; he saved all that for his girls.

Marianne's scream had been a siren call to his cock, it was harder, stiffer than it had been when he started the game. He couldn't get over how good she was at the yes/no game; he knew from the way she looked at him that her resistance was calculated to make his heart race and his slamming even harder. Harder and harder he pushed and when he was done, he lifted her gently asking her if she had enjoyed it.

'Yes, that was good, and I enjoyed it Mr Smithson.' Her voice was husky and he was tender.

After she left the music room, he had stopped by James' office to sound him out. Now that he'd conquered there was no reason for him to hang around. The other girls he had been cultivating didn't hold the same fascination to him as Marianne; it was the high he wanted to leave on.

'Good God man what the hell were you thinking?' James's response had been unexpected and Hugh thought, a little over-exaggerated after all, they were all up to it to some degree.

Calmly, he explained it again. 'I just thought you should know that I've had problems with Marianne Langley.' He looked at James, 'We've been having coffee regularly and I may have given her the wrong impression. She came on to me just now. I thought you should know as she might have a bruise or two where I pushed her off.'

James' eyes bulged. 'Her parents are some of the most influential we have.'

Ah yes, there it was Hugh thought. Concern for school reputation rather than pupil welfare, a common malady amongst the better public schools, and one he had used relentlessly to his advantage over the years.

'I hadn't realised.' He lied smoothly. 'I'm sorry. Look if it's of any help I'll resign now, you can say I have family matters to attend to. End of year isn't far off and, as long as I get a decent reference, I won't say anything about the matter either.' He was sure his offer would be accepted.

It was.

'It's such a shame, Hugh. You were one of the best German teachers we've ever had,' said James. 'It'll be hard to replace you.'

Holding out hands, they shook and parted friends.

A couple walked past him in the dark and his reverie was broken momentarily. Reaching into his pocket he took out a packet of cigarettes and put one in his mouth. Lighting it, he sucked in deeply, knowing they would assume he was just out for a crafty fag and not loitering, watching the windows in front of him.

Arms wrapped around each other; the presence of sex was unmistakable. He sniffed the air. They were both giving off the scent of recent bedroom pleasures and he wondered if the boy had learnt to play his girlfriend like the fine instrument she was.

That, he reflected, had always been his strength. He knew what women liked, had made it his business to learn everything there was to know about the art and desire of sex. As a teenager, he had poured over copies of the Karma Sutra with his mates, he had even found a copy of The Perfumed Garden in a local charity bring-and-buy sale, he was pretty sure the woman who sold it to him had no idea of its contents. If she had, he was certain she'd never have let it cross the threshold of the church hall.

He practised on himself, finding ways of holding off the moment of resolution as long as he could. When he took his girlfriend for the first time, she was convinced he was no virgin. He had been as confident as she was shy, despite the difference in their ages.

The only time he had varied his pattern had been with Sally. She had been out of the ordinary, driven as he'd been to punish Jenny for abandoning him, abandoning them.

After all, consensual sex was the most satisfying. But he had to admit there had been a rare pleasure in taking someone so violently. To know he had possessed her so totally her body, soul and mind had been his, was a triumph of sorts over all womanhood.

He had waited for the right moment with Sally, he didn't want to anticipate anything or make it too soon. He needed it to be when she was ripe, like a luscious, sweet peach, ready for the plucking. So he watched; visiting Dorset, parking in the layby getting the feel of the place a couple of times during each holiday period for two years.

Noting the comings and goings of the household and the neighbouring farm, it wasn't long before he found the barn. He realised it was rarely used and so perfectly suited to his needs.

Hugh had been ready the holiday before, but the opportunity never arose. The cold weather had kept the family indoors or transported around in cars. So, when the chance came, he took it, without thinking. All his planning had been done, the tape was ready, the block to lock the door. His final act was to sound the horn, providing a much-needed shock that would set the ball in motion. It had been fortuitous her bicycle chain had come off as well, a nice little accent fate had provided him.

She had been as sweet as anticipated. Leaving her body as she did allowed him to follow through on a fantasy he'd had for a long time of sex with someone who allowed him total domination over her.

Her eyes were open, but she didn't see him. Sitting on the bale, her legs across his thighs, he bounced gently and then more firmly, leaning back against the hay to allow him longer entry, he allowed her to ride him like a donkey, albeit one that required him to do all the work.

It had been, he reflected, rather like a weight training, but much more pleasurable.

Shaking his head, he broke away from his thoughts, realising the light in Laura's room had been out for some time and it was getting colder. Glancing at his watch, he realised he had been there over two hours, much longer than usual. It was time to go.

He had parked in a side street and when he reached the car, he noticed the girl diagonally opposite him glance in his direction. She didn't look like a hooker, but then you never could tell these days. He was aware of a tension in his midriff and a pleasant glow around his balls, it might be nice to get a quick one in before bed.

Swinging the car around expertly, he pulled up beside her. Stretching over the passenger seat he wound the window down.

'You looking for a ride?' he enquired winking.

She smiled back and pulled the passenger door open. 'It's fifty quid for the full job. Down to the end of the road and turn left, if you go to the end there's a car park, no one ever uses.' She instructed.

He did as she told him and pulling into the car park drove into the nearest convenient space.

'Back or front?' her question was direct.

Looking at her appraisingly, he tried to decide what type she was. 'Back I think.' Climbing out of the car. He walked around to the passenger side before she had a chance to get out and held out his hand. 'Madam' he said.

'Oh la la, I ain't had one like you before.' She smiled and took his hand before gracefully swinging her legs around to get off the seat.

She stood in front of the open back door. 'On or off?'

'Off, all of it.' His breath was coming in rasps, he was looking forward to something harder than usual.

Stepping out of her stilettos', she stripped off her top, bra, skirt, and knickers. Hands on hips she looked at him with a sardonic look on her face. 'And you, what you gonna take off?'

'Just this.' He said as he undid his trousers and boxers, pushing her down on the seat as he did so.

She opened her legs to him, holding them wide so he could enter her.

She was moist and he thrust his cock into her so hard she cried out.

'Shh, shh, not so noisy; we don't want anyone to hear.' He held a hand over her mouth as he hit into her harder, harder, harder; taking out years of watching 'his girls' without being able to touch them, on her.

When it was over, she gathered up her clothes and limped away from the car, struggling to pull her knickers on as she went. He laughed out loud watching her fall over in her rush to get away from him. She hadn't even asked him for the money.

He did his trousers up, straightened his shirt and brushed his hair back into place, he was satisfied. Turning the car engine over he drove past her slowly, looking her up and down in a derisory way, as if she wasn't good enough even to wipe her pussy on his boots.

She looked away. He thought she looked ashamed.

CHAPTER TWENTY-ONE

It was late when we woke the next morning.

Blearily, I opened her eyes and looked at the clock. 'My god Laura, get up, it's half past nine and we said we'd meet the parents at 10.00.'

Laura rolled over groaning. 'Do we have to, can't we just stay here in our nice cosy beds.' She snuggled down even further, complaining bitterly when I ripped the duvet off her.

'Gimme that back, that's not fair, I was all nice and warm.' She sat up indignant at so rude an awakening.

I was firm. 'Just get up Laura. We can pick up Sally, grab a coffee with the parents and some breakfast and then meet Marianne for that discussion we were talking about.'

That woke Laura up properly as she remembered the events of the previous evening.

'Oh yes, of course.' She scrambled out of bed and into last night's clothes saying 'I really must go and get changed into something other than a performance dress. I'll meet you in the quad, give me ten minutes.' And shot off through my door, hot-footing it back to her own room.

Breakfast was a leisurely affair at the hotel and all three sets of parents, and Jamie, were already seated when we arrived.

'Good morning darlings.' Laura's mother reached up to give her daughter a kiss.

'Go and get yourselves something to eat from the buffet.' My father instructed.

We all complied with the instruction, returning to the table with laden plates. 'Goodness, you're hungry.' My mother commented. 'I can't imagine eating that amount at this time in the morning'.

'I'm always starving the day after a performance and remember we're playing later in the church too; if you can make it.'

'We're all planning to be there.' Laura's father commented. 'This is the highlight of our year, and we don't want to miss a thing.'

We all smiled broadly. Our collective set of parents had always been so supportive of our chosen paths, too supportive in some ways it turns out, I thought ruefully.

Breakfast finished, I gathered up Sally and Laura saying to the others, 'There's some practice we need to do before tonight's performance in the church.'

Everyone nodded except for Jamie who mouthed, 'See you later?'

I nodded in acknowledgement.

We walked quickly to Marianne's hotel and after making ourselves known to reception were buzzed up to her room.

'Thank god you're here, I was wondering if you'd all forgotten.' Marianne gathered us into a giant hug.

'There was no chance of anyone forgetting.' Said Laura seriously.

'Did you sleep last night?' Asked Sally.

Laura and I laughed. 'We stayed together last night and kept each other awake with our snoring.'

Marianne looked tired. 'I hardly slept at all, the nightmares were worse than ever.'

Sally nodded in affirmation. 'I was the same. I kept going over and over in my head what had happened and I'm kicking myself I didn't see him.'

I reached out and patted her arm. 'Don't worry I saw him enough for both of us.'

Marianne opened her bedroom door. 'Shall we go and find a quiet spot in the bar for coffee? It might be better than crowding around on my bed.'

We all trooped out after her and down to the lobby and bar. We settled comfortably in a corner booth and ordered coffees all round.

I was the first to speak. 'I know I may have spoken out of turn, but I asked Jamie if he could be here today, I'd like him to know what's going on.' The look on Sally's face said it all. 'Look, Sal, I would have told him sooner if he'd been in the country, you must know that.'

Marianne said. 'I don't know whether that's a good idea or a bad idea because I still don't know how you all know Mr Smithson.'

'Mr Johnson', chimed in Laura, 'He was Mr Johnson to me.'

Sally, spoke quietly. 'Why don't we all tell our stories and then we can think about what to do next, at least that way we'll all know everything. And I'll go first if that's ok with you as I just want to get it over with.' We all nodded, and she began, hesitantly at first because telling someone something shocking for the first time is always hard.

Marianne's face was pale and shocked by the time Sally had finished. 'It's so awful, it doesn't bear thinking about.'

'I'll go next.' Said Laura who told her story in a straightforward, factual way with no emotion showing on her face at all.

'Do you want to tell us what happened to you Marianne before I tell you my story?' I offered, not out of any kindness but because I knew that what I had to say might be the most shocking of all.

Marianne nodded and proceeded to tell us everything that had led up to her rape and what had happened afterwards. 'I vowed then I'd never have anything to with men, and I haven't.' She finished.

The others all turned to me expecting me to take the floor.

I took a deep breath and talked, fully, for the first time about my relationship with Mr Smithson. I didn't hold back anything and carried on despite the mixed emotions I watched playing across their faces. It was hard, harder than anything I had ever had to say before. It was even harder than telling Jamie because at least he had sort of accepted it, even if he didn't understand it.

'I was young, that's all I can put it down to, I thought he cared about me, and I was experimenting as much as anything else. Because my parents were ok with me meeting him regularly, it seemed to give it a blessing, if that makes any sort of sick sense.'

'He had never been violent, and I did consent, it's only since meeting Laura and then hearing Sally's story that I've realised it was wrong and should never have happened.' I finished in a flurry aware of their silence.

I looked at Sally. 'That was why Jamie and I split up, he knew all that and couldn't come to terms with it.'

Laura sat back in her chair saying 'I knew you'd agreed to it, but you've never said it was that deep. Now I know why you never wanted to say anything to the police, it wasn't a problem for you.'

I nodded. 'You're right, it wasn't a problem; until later, when I understood more.'

Marianne was frowning. 'So let me get the timelines right then; I was the first because he was at Wetherby before he went to Jamieson's; that means you must have been second Jenny. You were third Laura before he moved on to Sally.' We nodded our agreement.

She looked at me carefully. 'I can sort of understand what happened to you. He was very attractive and the coffee did work after a fashion. I lowered my guard enough for him to then throw the blame on me and it's that I've been dealing with ever since.'

She held out her hand I grasped it holding onto my lifeline. 'It must have been hard realising it had all been a set-up and that you were simply another notch in the proverbial bedpost.'

I looked away, grateful for Marianne's support and yet ashamed of my own body at the same time.

Laura and Sally were still frowning. 'Do you think he became more violent because of what he'd had with you?' Laura asked the question I oped I'd never have to answer.

I nodded. 'I think so, yes. But then we'll never really know unless we talk to him and I'm certainly never going to put myself in that position again.'

Sally held out her hand to me as well. 'You know I've never blamed you don't you?'

I squeezed her hand in thanks and nodded, tears pricking my eyes, 'I know Sal, but you don't have to, I blame myself every day.' I began to cry and instantly hankies were handed over from all quarters.

I blew my nose hard. 'Thank you, I don't know what I'd do without friends like you.'

An hour had passed in our discussion and I was acutely aware that Jamie was waiting.

'Look we need to decide what we're going to do, and I need to go and talk to Jamie if that's alright with the rest of you.'

'I think we have enough to go to the police with.' Marianne was firm. 'We all recognise him, except Sal of course as she didn't see him, but I could identify him and so could both of you, that should count for something shouldn't it?' She held a hand out inviting other suggestions.

Laura looked away. 'We've tried that so many times, I've tried it and so has Jenny, but they never want to know.'

'But this time it's different.' Marianne insisted. 'This time we're all here together and we can even show that he has two different identities.'

I could see Laura was reluctant to go down what she felt was a fruitless path again, but I nudged her. 'Marianne's right you know, we do have so much more to go with now than before.'

Nodding slightly Laura gave her assent.

'I should really go and see Jamie first, this could take a long time and we can't forget the performance tonight either, it wouldn't do if we were late.' I didn't want him to leave without saying goodbye.

'How about we leave it until tomorrow? It's Sunday so it will be quiet and none of us are performing. The parents will be gone too.' Sally was thoughtful, looking around at all of us. 'I know we'd all like to resolve this right now, but one more day won't hurt, after all, we've been carrying this around for years.'

We all agreed; Laura because she wanted to avoid it, Marianne because she didn't want to be catapulted immediately back into the maelstrom of fighting the authorities and me because I just couldn't face telling the truth about my part in it all, admitting my complicity..

It was a little after one when I finally turned up at the hotel.

Jamie was in the bar with a book, and he looked up and smiled. 'I didn't think you were coming.' He spoke quietly but with a smile.

'Oh, I was always going to see you, Jamie.' I sat down.

'Do you want something to drink, or some tea or coffee perhaps?' He was half out of the chair.

'No thanks. Look can we go somewhere else I don't want either of our parents coming in.' I spoke lightly, but he must have heard the urgency in my voice.

'Okay, you wait here while I go and grab a jumper and put this book away. I'll be no more than five minutes, I promise.' I watched him take the stairs two at a time and sat back, fingers drumming on the arm of the chair.

He was back almost immediately and, grabbing my arm he pulled me out of the chair. 'I happen to know a nice little café; we could have something to eat if you want.'

Nodding I trailed along after him as he took into a maze of streets I had rarely ventured into, preferring the familiarity of the university precincts.

I loved it. 'I've never been here before.' When he finally ushered me into a tiny, dark-holed Italian restaurant.

'Mr Jamie, how nice to see you again, it's been a long time.' The owner greeted him like a long-lost friend with a kiss on both cheeks and a firm hug.

'It has Giorgio, it has and how are you and the lovely Maria, and the rest of the family?'

'They are all good Mr Jamie, all good. Now can I seat you and your lovely lady?' Giorgio showed us to a table in the corner.

'That's great Giorgio and thank you.' Jamie's smile was infectious and I found myself smiling along with it.

His Italian friend handed over the menus and a wine list and Jamie ordered a bottle of sparkling water for me and a pint of lager for himself.

'What's the problem then Jen? What was so urgent you couldn't tell me last night?' Jamie was impatient.

Before I could begin Giorgio served our drinks and then hovered waiting for our food order of two pizzas.

'I know about Sal.' I said.

'I sort of worked that one out.' Jamie spoke without rancour. 'What is it about Sal then, is there a problem?'

I tried to assess how he might take the news and gave up; it would just have to be however it was.

'There's no easy way to tell you this Jamie and please don't lose it.' I tried to prepare him, knowing there was no way to do so gently. 'But the man who raped Sal is Mr Smithson.' I waited for his reaction.

It was a slow burn. When the memories finally came together his fuse was short. 'What the hell do you mean Jenny?' He shouted and the other diners turned around to look.

He lowered his voice saying again 'What the hell do you mean? Are you actually telling me the guy you shagged at school is the same bloke who raped my sister?'.

I felt my face drain of colour and nodded. I held my hands up as if to protect myself 'And it gets worse ..' I started.

'How the hell could it get any worse?' Jamie jumped in before I could finish.

I reached out to touch his arm and he flinched back. Sighing I sat back again. 'It gets worse because he's also the Mr Johnson who attacked Laura. And he raped Marianne, you remember, the viola soloist you met last night.

Jamie subsided. His face stricken. 'God, I'm sorry Jenny, I'm so sorry'.

'I don't understand why now, why are you telling me this now?' He was confused and looked it.

'Because it all came to a head yesterday.' And before I could explain any further our pizzas arrived and we both looked at them, slightly sickened.

Giorgio had heard the outburst and was discreet. 'Is there anything else you would like?' We both shook our heads, and I'm sure he went back to his station with the certain knowledge that the majority of what he had just served would still be there when we left.

He was right, both of us tried to eat but the food, delicious as it was, seemed like cardboard in our mouths. I watched us play cat and mouse on our plates, cutting off small pieces before pushing them around as if that action alone would make the pizza disappear.

Jamie looked at me and must have noticed the strain in my face and he softened. 'So, what happened to bring it all up again.'

I looked down, twisting my hands together. 'Because he was there, in the audience last night and because he sent us all roses before the performance. We didn't know about Marianne until last night either. That's where I've been this morning, since breakfast, talking. All of us have been talking about what to do. And I could really do with a friend who's not been touched by him right now.' And I knew my voice was small.

I took Jamie's hand when he offered it.

'I'm sorry I shouted Jenny, it's just you brought back all the memories of when we were together and the arguments we had. I never imagined it could be as bad as this and I didn't realise how much it might have hurt you too. I'm sorry, can you forgive me?' His voice was quiet and sincere.

I looked at him fully for the first time and saw such compassion there. 'There's nothing to forgive Jamie. Ever since I found out about Laura, and then Sal, I've realised it was all wrong, that it should never have happened and even though I know he's the one to blame, I still blame myself for being a stupid, stupid fool who was taken in by a predator.' I looked down. 'And I blame myself for Sally too, if it hadn't been for me then he would never have known about her and it would never have happened and I'm so sorry'.

'How long have you been holding all this blame and shame, Jenny?'

He spoke quietly and I could almost see the walls he'd built around his heart beginning to crack.

'I'm sure Sal doesn't blame you Jenny; I know I don't. You might be the link, but it wasn't you who did anything to her. You couldn't have known what would happen.'

I was grateful for his reassurance and ate another piece of pizza, forcing it down with water.

'Thanks, Jamie, I do appreciate you saying that.'

Jamie sat back on the seat and stared at the ceiling. 'What did you decide then, what did you all decide to do today when you talked?'

'We're going to the police. This time we think we have enough for them to do something about it. He's been stalking Laura for years, turning up at all her performances. He's probably done the same to all of us but the rest of us aren't as interested in the audience as Laura is so have never noticed. Last night was the first time I'd seen him and that was when Laura and I made the connection, that he was the same man.'

'I'm not sure what help I can be but would you like me to come with you, I can provide some moral support or pizza?' He half-joked.

I shook my head. 'No, I don't think so, but it's good to have you as a friend again?' The question must have been apparent in my voice as Jamie nodded quickly.

'Always, Jen, always.'

CHAPTER TWENTY-TWO

Jamie insisted on walking me back to my room.

At the entrance, he gave me a bear hug. 'If there's anything I can do just let me know, you can call me in Dorset, I'm going to be around for a few weeks anyway.'

I nodded and hugged him back.

He stood watching her as she walked up the stairs before heading over to his sister's halls.

'Jenny told me what happened Sal.' He was matter of fact.

She nodded and pulled the door wider, inviting him in. 'Tea, coffee, coke?' she offered. 'I don't have anything stronger I'm afraid Jamie.'

He shook his head. 'Jenny and I had a pizza together so a coke would be good.'

Sally walked down to the kitchen, dawdling, she didn't want to face what was coming.

'Here you go.' She handed him the can and opened her own.

'So, she told you everything then Jamie?' It was rhetorical more than a question.

'Yes, she told me everything. The only thing I don't get though Sal, is the name. You always said you didn't know his name.' Jamie looked at her directly, challenging her to deny it.

'You're right.' She sighed. 'It was the one thing I never said to anyone, because it didn't feel 'right' somehow like it wasn't his real name. But I do remember him telling me I could call him Mr Smithson. And I was right, his name isn't Mr Smithson and I bet it's not Mr Johnson either.' She was fierce in her reasoning, challenging him in return to say she wasn't right.

Jamie pushed his hands through his hair and sighed. 'You have to tell someone you know that don't you Sal?'

'I will Jamie, tomorrow we're all going to the police with it and who knows, if he's at another performance then we may just be able to catch him.' She said it lightly, although her heart was beating fast. She hoped he wouldn't be there, didn't know what might happen to her performance if he was.

Jamie looked up understanding that of course, if he'd been stalking them for years, it would make sense, he'd be at tonight's concert too. Making his mind up. 'I'm coming tonight, I'll keep an eye out.'

Sally smiled, reassured that her brother was looking out for her. 'Thanks, Jamie, that would be good, and I know we'd all feel safer.'

'I'm going to call Davey as well. I think we might stand a better chance if there are more of us about.'

Sally nodded 'If you think that would help. It would be nice to see Davey. I haven't heard from him since Christmas.'

'You know Davey, keeps us all guessing'. Jamie smiled.

Miriam and Jeremy were surprised to see their middle child turn up unexpectedly mid-afternoon.

'Hi Pop's, how are you?' He gave his father a firm hug'.

'Hey Ma, where's Jamie?' He pulled his mother close and kissed her cheek.

'What a lovely surprise, I didn't know you were coming down to see the concert tonight darling.' She exclaimed.

'Last minute thing you know. Just happened to have a free night and thought it would be good to get out and do something different for the evening.' He smiled encouragingly, 'Jamie?'

'Oh yes, he's up in his room, 217. Are you staying with him, I think it's got two doubles.' She said.

'Thanks, Ma.' As he headed for the stairs, taking them, as Jamie did, two at a time.

'Well, what a nice surprise Jeremy, did you know anything about it?' Miriam asked her husband and he, being as in the dark as she shook his head and carried on reading the paper.

'Give.' Davey ordered when Jamie had let him into his room. 'What's going on that I had to find an excuse to leave work early and drop a date. It had better be good, or else.' He laughed to show the threat was an empty one.

Fifteen minutes later he was as serious-faced as Jamie had been when he walked in.

'What, all four of them attacked by this one bloke?' Davey could hardly believe what Jamie had told him. 'It sounds like the plot of some dreadfully poor TV drama rather than real life. You couldn't make it up if you tried.' He was incredulous.

Stretching over his brother he grabbed another beer. 'At least that explains what happened to you and the lovely Jenny. He glanced at Jamie. 'Look, I'm sorry, it sounds like it's been hard on you both.' He punched Jamie affectionately on the arm.

Jamie tried to look cool about it but failed. 'It was tough, and I don't think I handled it very well either. Knowing what I know now I feel like a real cad for letting her cope with it all on her own; and Sal too for that matter.' He pushed his hair out of his eyes again and looked at his brother.

At six foot four, his brother had surpassed him in height; but they both had strong physiques, the result of hours spent in the gym.

'What do you reckon anyway, do you think we could take him down between us if we tried?' Jamie asked his brother.

'Only if we know what the bastard looks like. We can't just pick on any random guy who happens to be sitting alone in a pew, can we.' Davey's point was well made. 'Have any of them given you a good description of him?'

'Sal and Jenny seem to be the most similar, but it looks like along with the names he's changed his style over the years too. I've asked Sally to work out a way of letting us know where he is if he turns up. She'll tell just before the performance starts tonight.'

Davey nodded. 'That sounds like the best plan we've got, what will we do with him when we grab him though?'

That was the bit Jamie was still a bit hazy about. 'The girls have said they want to go to the police so how about we frogmarch him down there for them, save the police the effort of trying to find him.' Jamie suggested.

'Well, it's full of holes, but if they don't want to do anything about it until after the performance, we don't have much choice really.' They chinked cans and sat back in their seats, each lost in their thoughts.

We were all in the practice room when Sally told the others in quiet tones. 'Jamie and Davey are both in the audience.'

Marianne looked confused. 'Davey?'

'My other brother.' Sal explained.

'Ah.' Said Marianne.

Laura was pleased, it had been a long time since she'd seen Davey. She still remembered fondly the Christmas kiss they'd shared at the beginning of her university days.

Sally caught the look. 'He's a year younger than you, surely you want someone your own age.'

'Never say never Sal.' Laura replied. 'And anyway, what's a year or two in a relationship? As you get older it hardly matters.'

Sally and I looked at each other raising our eyebrows in mock exasperation. We'd both watched with fascination the sexual tension between Laura and Davey whenever they happened to fall into common plans.

'I said to Jamie I'd let him know where he was sitting if he comes, so we need to agree on something we can all do without interrupting the performance or being spotted.'

They all thought hard.

'How about I point my bow.' Offered Laura.

I looked at her in disgust. 'And that's discreet, is it?'

Laura looked shamefaced. 'Well, perhaps not.'

Sally's face lit up. 'I think I've got it.' We looked at her eagerly. 'How about Laura drops a hanky and bends to pick it up in the direction he's sitting. There can't be many single men sat in the audience after all.'

Marianne wasn't the only one to look disappointed. 'If that's the best we can come up with then I suppose it will have to do.'

'It is difficult to do something that doesn't interrupt anything. I'll go and see Jamie and let him know. And Laura, make sure you've got that hanky stuffed up your sleeve or somewhere handy.' Sally dashed off to catch up with her brothers and tell them of the plan they'd come up with.

Jamie and Davey looked as disappointed as we had felt.

'Is that the best you could do between you? Brains the size of universes and you come up with a hanky.' Davey was scathing.

'Short of rising to our feet, pointing at him and saying, "Stop him", yes that's the best we can do. We can't interrupt the performance or alert him.' Sally was less than pleased at the reaction and turned to Jamie.

'Are you ok with this as a plan Jamie? Do you think it has a chance of working?'

Jamie shrugged his shoulders. 'I don't know, but if it's what we've got then we'll make the best of it, won't we Davey?' He punched his brother on the shoulder and Davey nodded.

The audience filed into the Church. It was small but had perfect acoustics for its many informal musical recitals. I waved to my parents and the other family members as they sat down. Straining my neck I could just make out Jamie and Davey sat in the last pews on opposite sides of the aisle.

I looked at the rest of the audience. Normally I would ignore them as I spent the last few moments preparing mentally for the experience of letting music consume me, bringing myself under control. This time, however, I found it a struggle to concentrate, and my eyes roamed around trying to locate Mr Smithson.

I noticed our conductor bring his baton up and look at me pointedly. Sitting straighter in my chair I nodded, and we began.

The performance ended an hour and thirty minutes later. I was exhausted from playing the double act of musician and amateur sleuth. As far as I could tell he wasn't in the audience and when I looked at Laura seated on the opposite side the small shake of her head confirmed her fears. He hadn't turned up, Jamie and Davey had a wasted trip.

'Never mind.' They both said later. 'It doesn't matter, perhaps it's all over.'

But Laura shook her head vehemently. 'He's playing a game. He's never missed any performance that I know of, except this one. I wonder why that might be, Jenny?' Her comment was barbed, and I flinched back from it.

I flung my hands up. 'If he knew we were planning something then what could we do? I wasn't aware of anyone watching me, but I certainly didn't keep it a secret I was meeting Jamie either.'

'There's no point in arguing ladies.' Jamie said peaceably. 'He might have been ill, he might not like the repertoire, or he could be watching someone else. Anything could have changed his mind for all we know, so let's not play the blame game.'

We both subsided, each to her corner of the imaginary boxing ring.

'Why don't we go and get a drink.' Suggested Davey. 'We can think about what we're going to do next.'

'I know exactly what I'm going to do next.' Stormed Laura. 'I'm going to the police, as we agreed, in the morning. Hopefully, you're all coming with me.' She glared at the rest of us, challenging us to back down.

Marianne held up her hand. 'Laura, we all agreed to go to the police tomorrow, we'd have done that anyway, regardless of what had happened tonight, although I'm not quite sure what would have happened tonight?' She looked quizzically at Jamie and Davey.

Jamie gave her a rueful smile. 'Well.' He drew it out. 'We hadn't actually got a concrete plan other than to grab him.' He looked at Davey, who shrugged. 'To tell the truth, we were flying by the seat of our pants.'

He continued. 'But if you lovely ladies would like some company down at the police station tomorrow, Davey and I will be happy to escort you, won't we.' He nudged Davey sharply in the ribs.

Davey nodded. 'Sure, of course.'

'Right.' Jamie rubbed his hands together. 'Let's get a drink and then see you all back to your various rooms and we can all catch up again in the morning. So, who's first?'

'Actually, we.' I indicated myself, Sally, and Laura. 'Need to see the parents first, so if you don't mind Marianne, the boys can take you back to the hotel now, if that's ok with you.'

Marianne smiled. 'Of course. I was going to suggest it. I'll send them right back as soon as I'm safely through the hotel door.' She waved, and the three walked off into the evening.

We three caught up with our parents in the pub opposite the Church. Once again there was praise from them all for our performances and compliments ranging from stunning to beautiful to fantastic. We all smiled, knowing our parents were always our biggest cheerleaders.

'Thanks, Mum.' I said. 'It means such a lot that you and Dad come for all the concerts.'

My mother smiled and patted my arm. 'We both adore hearing you play and I'm just sorry that Dad's work takes us away so much otherwise, we'd be here permanently.'

Dad drew me into another bear hug. 'You are something special Jennifer Bean. Anything you need, anything you want, any time at all, you just have to call, you do know that don't you?' He regarded me seriously. 'We know something's going on sweetheart and we know you don't want to talk about it right now, but if there's ever a problem you don't know how to deal with all you have to do is ask.'

He hugged me more tightly and I returned the embrace, tears pricking the back of my eyes. 'Thank you Daddy.' I looked down. 'I will tell you, we'll all tell you when the time is right, but it's not just now.' I held his hand. 'Is that ok?'

'Of course, it is sweetheart. It doesn't mean we don't worry, but we won't interfere.' He turned back to the other parents. 'Right, who would like what to drink?'

Jamie and Davey were back a few minutes later.

Drawing me to one side, Jamie pulled me into a deep hug. He sighed.

'Jen.' He started, 'I know we haven't exactly been..' He struggled to find the right words. '.. the best of friends lately, but I've missed you. I've missed this.' He flung his arm around the group. 'Would you consider having dinner with me when the festival's over?' He added hastily.

I was thoughtful. 'I'd love to Jamie. But the whole mess that caused our problems in the first place is still there. It's never going to go away you know, however this ends.' I held my breath waiting to see what he said next.

'I know all that Jenny, I honestly do and of course it matters. It matters a lot that you and Sally have a connection that can never be broken, that's bigger than us. But, knowing what I know now, it feels different. You didn't have a choice. I can see that now.' He held his hand up as I started to protest. 'No you didn't. If you hadn't been how you were it could have been so much worse, look at Marianne, Sal and Laura. Funnily, I think you protected yourself.'

I regarded him slightly confused. 'I'd never thought of it like that before. Thank you, it casts a different light on it, one that doesn't have me playing the fool.'

'Dinner then?' Jamie asked the question again.

'Yes please, thank you, I'd love to Jamie, I'd love to do that.' I smiled, my heart felt all lit up inside and peace descended for the first time in a long time.

'So, what have you been up to since Christmas then Laura?' Davey asked the question offhandedly, not expecting much of a reply.

Laura looked at him. 'Oh this and that, you know. Lots of practice of course and finishing up course work. The end of the year beckons, and finals start in a couple of weeks.'

Davey nodded. 'I'm so glad I decided to avoid all that palaver and head straight out into the world of work, so much more satisfying and financially viable. Who'd be a struggling student.' He winced when Sally thumped him.

'What did you do that for?' He asked aggrieved.

'We don't exactly struggle you know. Mummy and Daddy, and Laura's and Jen's parents all give generously in the cause of great art.' She laughed. 'Don't look so downhearted Davey, you too could have had an easy life of lectures, exams, and pressure if you'd wanted it.'

'Not flippin' likely Sal.' He said. 'It's so much easier out in the real world you know.'

'What exactly do you do then Davey?'. Laura was intrigued. 'I don't think you've ever really explained it.'

Davey turned to her and gestured to a seat. 'Let's sit down and I'll explain.'

He slid his arm around the back of her and let his hand rest lightly on her shoulder whispering in her ear. 'It's like this see, I take money and give it to other people. In return, they give me a bit of money back.'

She hit him playfully. 'There's no need to be patronising you know, I do understand the basic concepts of banking.'

He laughed and pulled her closer. She didn't resist.

After drinks had been finished Jamie and Davey gathered us all up to escort us back to halls. Calls of 'see you in the morning' and 'catch you at breakfast' were shared between parents and children as each group went their separate ways.

Davey had his arm loosely around Laura, and Jamie was holding my hand.

'I feel like a spare part.' Complained Sally. 'It's like being the only one in the back row of the cinema without a boyfriend.'

We all laughed. 'One day Sally, one day.' Said Laura.

'Nope, not likely, never.' Sally was vehement in her objection.

CHAPTER TWENTY-THREE

Breakfast at the hotel the following morning was busy and noisy. The families had gathered for one last time before departure.

Over coffee, my father reminded me what he'd said the previous evening. 'I don't want to know what's going on darling, I just need to know you're safe.' He ventured.

I hugged him. 'It's fine daddy. It's under control and anyway, I have Jamie to look after me'.

He looked at me quizzically. 'I thought that was over?'

'It was, but maybe now it's not.' I smiled and looked across the table to the object of our discussion, who smiled back and waved.

'I must admit I'll be much happier knowing you two are seeing each other again. I've always said there's nothing that boy wouldn't do for you, and I know he would never let you down.'

'You're right Dad, he won't let me down. And now, it's time to go and time for you..' I gestured to the parents. '.. all to go home too. It's been so good to see you Mummy, and I'll see you soon, right after finals are finished.'

My mother took a delicate lace handkerchief out of her handbag and dabbed at her eyes. 'It's been lovely to see you too darling and I'm so proud of you. You've turned into such an accomplished musician and a wonderful young woman too.'

I blushed. 'Thanks, Mum'. I couldn't help wondering if she would feel the same when she found out what had been happening in my life all these years and how it had all started.a

Laura and Sally both rose from their seats, along with Jamie and Davey. Hugs were shared all around and promises to visit over the long summer ahead were given.

'We'll see you all, and Marianne, in Dorset at the beginning of July.' Said Miriam and we nodded looking forward to beginning our musical ensemble.

The door to the police station swung open and all six of us walked in.

The officer behind the desk glanced up. 'How can I help you?'

'Well.' I began, assuming the role of spokesperson. 'We'd like to see someone about a man who has been following us all and who has attacked us too.' I wasn't quite sure how to put it without it seeming outlandish and bizarre.

The desk sergeant regarded us critically. 'Take a seat over there and someone will be out to speak to you shortly.' He pointed to a row of plastic chairs, screwed together like a chain gang.

We sat feeling uncomfortably like we were being scrutinised unfavourably from the other side of the lobby. I watched him as he glanced over at us while speaking quietly into the phone. He nodded once and we started to rise, he gestured us back down again. 'The duty officer is coming out to see you shortly.'

We collapsed back into our seats with a collective sigh. There was nothing to do but look at the walls, the ceiling, through the plate glass doors. Jamie held my hand tightly. 'It'll be alright, don't worry.' He whispered.

'We've been here so many times before and nothing has been done before. I can't help feeling we're wasting our time, again.' My voice sounded low and depressed. I could feel disappointment rising yet again.

Smiling encouragingly, he grasped my hand even tighter.

Some twenty minutes later an efficient-looking head poked around the door to the lobby. 'Are the people who reported someone suspicious?' It said.

We nodded in unison and the door opened wider.

A young policewoman came through and beckoned us to follow her, calling 'Thanks Bob, I've got them.' Back to the desk sergeant who nodded tersely.

'Sit down, if you can.' She gestured at the two chairs in front of the desk. Sally and Marianne were quickest off the mark and the rest of us stood shuffling our feet behind.

'How can I help you?'

Laura pushed me forward. 'You tell her.' She instructed.

I began hesitantly. 'It's a bit difficult, I don't actually know where to start.'

'Why don't you try at the beginning.' The policewoman said kindly. 'It's usually the best place.'

I nodded and cleared my throat. 'Ok.' I took a deep breath. 'When I was 15 a teacher at my school molested me, had sex with me.' I paused, allowing that to sink in. 'It turns out the same teacher also raped Marianne and Sally and tried to attack Laura too.' I stopped and regarded the policewoman.

'Okay.' The officer said. 'Anything else?'

I couldn't help being put off by her matter-of-fact tone, I'd expected her to be at least a little interested.

'There is. He's been following us, standing outside Laura's room most nights and mine at least once. And he turns up at our performances too. On Friday, he sent us all roses.' Even to my ears, it sounded implausible.

The policewoman nodded; she was writing things down.

'What's his name, this teacher of yours?'

I felt uncomfortable. 'That's the problem, we don't really know.'

The policewoman looked confused. 'But I thought you said he was your teacher?'

'He was.' I agreed. 'But when I knew him, he was called Hugh Smithson, the same with Marianne. And we think the same with Sally but can't be sure. When Laura knew him, he was called Johnson.' I shrugged.

'How do you know it's the same person?' It was a perfectly reasonable question, but I squirmed.

'Well, we all saw him, on Friday, at the performance. That is, we all saw him except Sally. We only connected the dots after that.'

The policewoman turned to Sally. 'And you didn't see him?'

Sally shook her head, embarrassed.

'So how can you say it's the same man?'

Sally looked like she was about to cry so I started to speak for her. The policewoman held her hand up. 'No, I need to hear it from Sally. Sally, can you tell me why you didn't see him?'

Looking up at the ceiling, Sally said. 'I just didn't notice him, that's all. But I know he's the same man because the man who raped me told me his name was Mr Smithson, and that's the name of the man who abused Jenny. it's got to be the same person.'

The policewoman smiled thinly. 'The problem is that there could be dozens, hundreds of men called Smithson, we can't make that assumption I'm afraid.'

I heard Marianne, who had been listening to the exchange with increasing frustration, let out a deep sigh.

'Do you have something to add, Miss ...' The policewoman said pointedly.

'Marianne, Marianne Langley.' She offered. The policewoman noted it down on her pad. 'Look, Friday was the first time I'd seen that monster since he'd raped me at school. Hearing what I have from the other girls, knowing he's still out there and watching us is frightening. In fact, I'm terrified he's going to do it again. What I'd like to know is what you plan to do about it?'

The policewoman shushed her with her hand. 'Miss Langley, there is no need to take that tone and I have written down everything you have all said. Now, I need you all to give me an accurate description of the man you call Mr Smithson or Mr Johnson, or whatever his name is. Only when I have that can we decide what we intend to do about it.' She glared at us.

'Right, you can do it here, now; or you can come back; which is it to be?'

We all looked at each other and silently nodded. 'We'll do it now, thank you.' I spoke for all of us.

'Ok, let me get you some paper and pens and I'll leave you to it.' The officer left the room.

Laura was the first to explode. 'It's like she didn't believe us.' She folded her arms angrily. 'I thought this time we'd have a chance of getting rid of him for good, fat chance of that happening.' Davey tried to soothe her, but she shrugged him off.

'We'll get the descriptions done and then see what happens from there.' I offered. 'We don't know what might happen, you never know he might match a description they've already got.'

Sally started. 'You mean, you don't think we're the only ones?' It was obviously something she hadn't considered.

'Not the first and definitely not the last.' I confirmed grimly.

We stumbled out of the police station three hours later, subdued and beaten by the system we had thrown ourselves into.

'Anyone fancy a drink?' Asked Jamie. 'I don't know about you but all that time without even an offer of water is inhuman.'

We all nodded in agreement and followed his lead to the nearest pub.

When we were settled in a corner, we started to dissect what had just happened.

Marianne sighed. 'It was the same when I reported what happened to me to the head. He just laughed it off too, saying that I'd led Mr Smithson on, that it was all my own fault. He said at the time the police wouldn't be interested and I can see now how right he was.'

'Me and Jenny have been through the same rigmarole several times over the years, whenever I've tried to report him to the police.' Laura agreed.

We sat glumly looking at the bottom of our glasses.

'Maybe, this is just something we need to deal with ourselves then.' I suggested lightly. 'If the police won't help us, can't help us as they claim, then perhaps we just have to take matters into our own hands.'

Jamie looked sceptical. 'And what exactly did you have in mind, Agatha? We found out on Friday we aren't exactly cut out to be amateur detectives.'

'And what would you do with him if you caught him?' Asked Davey, 'Jamie and I didn't think that bit through either.'

I thought about it for a minute. 'Kill him.' I said simply.

Even volatile Laura looked shocked. 'You can't possibly be serious Jenny'.

'I can and I am. If no one else is going to help us, then we need to help ourselves.' I was firm.

'But killing someone, that's big stuff, Jenny. It means prison, all sorts of things, you can't even imagine what might happen if you take that step.' Sally put her hand out to me. 'You don't mean it.'

'I do and even if you don't join me then I'll do it myself.' I laid my head in my hands. 'The guilt and shame I feel every single day of my life is killing me. Because of me, he attacked you, Sally. That's something I have to live with forever.'

'Don't make it worse by taking a life, Jenny, the guilt over that will be far bigger and have many more consequences than how you feel about what happened to me.' Sally spoke quietly holding my hand.

'Oh, I don't know, it's all too much.' And my tears flowed freely once again. 'We need to end this. And we're trying the ways we're supposed to but they seem closed to us. They're empty of the solutions we need and I'm tired of waiting until he pulls his next stunt.'

'We don't know who he is, what he's done, where he's been and how many women he's attacked. We don't know if he's murdered anyone. Look at what happened to Sally, he's certainly capable of it. I dare you to disagree.' I stared the rest of them down. 'I dare you to say that I'm not right.' I was willing them to show me the flaw in what I was saying, but they couldn't.

I looked at them all darkly. 'Perhaps, just perhaps what I've said is exactly what he's planning.'

CHAPTER TWENTY-FOUR

I stretched my arms and hands above my head and let the sun beat down on them. Turning slightly, I looked at Laura lying next to me, she was asleep. Turning to the other side I watched Sally curled up in a foetal position, also asleep. Propping myself up on both elbows I looked towards my feet and Marianne who sat with her back against the old elm tree busily sucking the end of a pen.

'What are you thinking?' I asked in a low voice.

Marianne looked up surprised. 'I thought you were asleep, like the others.' She indicated Laura and Sally.

'There's too much going on in my head for that I'm afraid.' I admitted. 'All I do is lie with my eyes closed, hoping that somehow sleep is going to drop on me like a big cosy blanket, but it never does.'

Marianne nodded in agreement. 'I understand. Every time I close my eyes I see that barn.' she indicated with her head in the general direction of the road. 'And think 'That could have been me'. She sighed. 'Will it ever stop do you think, this watchful waiting?'

I sat up properly 'I don't know' I was as honest as I could be. 'I hope so, but something like this shapes you, moulds you and regardless of what happens, it will never leave you, not completely.' I looked at Marianne. 'It can't can it, after all it's as much a part of what makes you as..' I waved around '.. 'well, you.' I smiled lamely.

Marianne smiled. 'I think I sort of know that.' She was thoughtful for a moment. 'But will the nightmares stop? The fear I feel every time I close the curtains at night, the horror I endure at the thought he might break in, is watching me, wondering what he's thinking and why.'

I got up and flopped down against the tree next to her and hugged her close. 'They will, in time.' I made the promise even though I wasn't entirely sure of my facts about that.

'What are you two going on about?' Laura had woken up. 'Are you being all philosophical again Jen?'

I laughed. 'Philosophical me? I didn't know you knew the meaning of the word.'

Laura stretched out one long leg in a vain attempt to kick me, but the gap between us was too wide.

'Come closer so I can kick you.' She demanded instead.

'No way Laura, you look like you want to do some serious damage.'

Laura looked fierce. 'You were talking about him again, weren't you?'

We shook our heads innocently.

'I know you were it's written all over your faces.' She sat up. 'I'm going to remind you Miss Jennifer Hunter of some very wise words you said to me once, a long, long time ago now. You said..' Laura pointed at me. '.. you said not to allow him to take over, to put what he'd taught me about discipline in the face of anything to good use and not let his presence in the audience be anything other than a naughty child trying to distract me when I was busking.' She stopped. 'Do you remember that conversation, Miss Hunter? Do you?'

I looked down. 'You're quite right Laura, I did say all those things and I meant them at the time, but now.' I waved my arms around helplessly. 'Everything seems to have changed.'

'What's changed exactly, tell me that, Jenny?' Laura demanded. 'Nothing, nothing is what's changed. We know no more about him, what he's doing, why he did what he did than we did back then. If we let this take over like you two are doing right now, then he's won, right.' The challenge was evident in her voice.

'Do you seriously want to live your lives in fear, too afraid of your own shadow to do anything, too scared to venture out alone?' She was scathing, 'I know I don't, and I'll take the consequences of what happens.'

Looking at Sally, she continued. 'It didn't stop Sally going to St Cecilia's. It didn't stop her from going to uni, did it? She's one of the bravest people I know.'

Sally stirred. 'What?' She mumbled. 'What did you say Laura?'

Laura patted her arm. 'Nothing Sal, nothing at all you need to worry about.' And Sally returned to slumber.

Marianne and I looked at each other. Marianne spoke for us both. 'You're right, you often are you know Laura. But I haven't learnt the art of putting it to one side yet, I never received the 'training' you and Jenny did, so I don't know how to forget him.'

'I never said forget him, we can't do that, what I said was to put him to one side.' Laura looked at me with a grin. 'How might we go about teaching Marianne to put distractions aside without it being slightly sadistic?'

Marianne looked worried. 'If either of you so much as lay one finger on me in any way that suggests girl-on-girl sex, I'll be out of this place so damn fast you won't see me move.'

I laughed. 'Stupid woman, there are other ways you know, and they don't have to involve someone fingering you. Get up, get up from where you are.' I pulled her arm to join me. 'Now turn and turn to face the tree.' I encouraged her to turn round.

Marianne did as she was told but I could see she was apprehensive about what we were going to do next.

'Imagine you have your voila in hand and you're about to play.' I thought for a moment. 'Bach, the Gamba Sonatas'.

Marianne raised her arms holding an imaginary instrument and bow. 'Ok, I've got that in my mind.'

'Right, now play it, hear it in your head, feel the music.' I instructed.

Marianne started to move in time to her internal recording, and when she became lost in the piece her fingers moved lightly over the 'viola' and her bow movements were strong and sure, Laura crept up behind and touched her lightly on the back.

Marianne jumped. 'What did you do that for?' She demanded dropping her imaginary instruments.

'That's what you need to learn.' Said Laura. 'When you've mastered the art of ignoring whatever we might do then you'll stand a chance of putting him out of mind whenever you want to.'

Marianne looked at us. 'Do you mean to tell me, that's what the pair of you went through at every practice for .. how long?'

We both nodded. 'But it was worse than that.' I said. 'Remember he was touching us in places he shouldn't have been at the same time.' I looked down. 'It teaches you a lot that sort of practice.'

Marianne reached over and stroked us both gently on the arm. 'I'm so sorry, I had no idea.'

'Have I missed something?' Sally had woken up.

'Not much that you'd notice.' Said Laura, smiling at us both. We were just teaching Marianne the finer points of managing an ignorant audience.

'Ah yes, I remember those lessons well.' Sally said pointedly. 'She.' Pointing at me. 'Made me stand and play while she threw little sponges at me. Hours it went on.' She paused. 'Well it seemed like hours at the time, I'm sure it probably wasn't.'

'Mmm, I'm beginning to get a sense of just how sadistic these two can be if they put their minds to it. I wouldn't want to be on the wrong side of them.' Marianne agreed.

We all laughed.

Sally looked up at the sky, shading her eyes from the sun. 'It's too hot to do anything, I certainly couldn't bear to practice in this heat. How about we all head down to the beach for a swim?'

We nodded enthusiastically. 'Sounds like a great idea.' Said Laura who was busy gathering up the blankets and heading back indoors.

It didn't take long to persuade Mrs Jones to make up a picnic and put together what we needed for swimming. Within 30 minutes we were in Marianne's car and heading to the beach, singing for all our worth with Cher to the Shoop Shoop song on the radio. Windows down and waving our hands out of the windows.

Despite the heat, the beach was relatively empty. The long summer holiday hadn't started for schools yet and holidaymakers in their caravans still hadn't arrived in anything other than drips and drabs.

Laying out towels in a semi-circle we stretched out and prepared to brown.

'Do you know, we still don't have a name for ourselves.' Laura said suddenly. 'We can't just advertise ourselves as four musicians, can we?'

'How about four musicians and a secret?' I suggested.

Sally looked at me. 'That's brilliant Jenny, why don't we call ourselves that? It has a good ring to it.' Her hands marked the top of the bill in the air. 'Presenting, for one night only, Four musicians and a secret.'

I laughed. 'I don't think so Sally, we're classical players, and it sounds a bit daft.'

'I don't think so.' Marianne interjected. 'I agree with Sally, it's not your ordinary sort of name. And anyway, did you have anything better in mind?' She challenged.

I thought for a moment wondering how to broach the name I'd been mulling over for a few days. 'How about the Sabines?' Laura looked quizzical. 'You know as in the rape of ' I didn't bother finishing the sentence and took a deep breath. 'Or what about Raptio?'

Laura looked even more confused. 'Raptio?' she repeated. 'Is that even a real word?'

I nodded. 'It is, it's Latin for rape.' I was aware that they were staring at me. 'It also has other meanings like rapture, which is what we'd like people to feel when they listen to us.'

My friends looked doubtful.

'It's a bit weird, isn't it?' Sally said. 'Naming ourselves after what we've been through, wouldn't we be reminding ourselves all the time about that, whenever we saw the name of the quartet?'

'And what about when people ask us what it means..' added Laura. '.. what would we say to them?'

Marianne looked at me. 'Why do you think it matters that we call ourselves something so, so ..' She struggled for the word. '… disturbing Jenny?'

I sat up properly. 'I have a plan, and it fits with the plan and, it just feels right to recognise what brought us all together, as a group I mean. Just because the act itself was so destructive, doesn't mean what we create out of it should be anything other than positive.' I shrugged my shoulders indifferently. 'But it's up to all of us to agree on a name'.

The others looked at each other.

'Well, I don't have any ideas, do either of you?' Asked Laura

Marianne and Sally both shook their heads.

'Although I do still like four musicians and a secret.' Said Sally with a wink.

'Why don't we relax now and think about it, see how we all feel later, when we get back indoors.' Marianne's suggestion was met with nods. 'In the meantime ..' She held her glass and a bottle up. '... glass of wine anyone and Jenny can tell us what this plan of hers involves.'

The others stretched over with their glasses and I settled back satisfied it had gone better than expected. I was ready to share my ideas.

'I'd like you to sit back and listen carefully, as I shall say zis only vonce.' I said in my best French accent.

The others rolled their eyes and lay down as I painted a picture of the plan I had in my mind, in theirs.'

By the end, Marianne was impressed. 'That might just work, but it's going to take a while, isn't it? We're never going to have all that knowledge inside a year are we?'

'And while we're doing that, he's still out there, doing whatever he's doing and getting away with it.' Said Laura.

Sally disagreed. 'I think it's a great idea. It's going to take time, maybe a few years, but if we believe we're laying out a trail of cheese crumbs for a mouse then I'm happy to go along with the game. Because that's what it feels like, a game.' She held up her hand to prevent their excuses. 'I know it's got high stakes, but this way we're taking back some control over what happens.'

Laura grumbled. 'I don't know, I don't like it, it's risky and dangerous. You've said yourself, Jenny. We don't know what he's capable of and what if we raise the stakes so high we put ourselves at even more risk?'

'I agree with Laura.' Said Marianne. 'But I am prepared to give it a go, as long as we all promise to call in help if it gets out of hand?' She looked at us all pointedly.

'I would do that anyway.' I agreed. And besides we'll have Jamie and Davey to help. And we're going to watch each other like hawks, all the time, no respite I'm afraid. I'm pretty sure he would never attack more than one of us at a time. If we're always together then we've got safety in numbers. Remember, we'll be working together in our new quartet so we'll spend a lot of time together anyway.' I thought for a moment. 'It might be a good idea if we shared a house. We get to practice when we want and it means no one ever needs to be alone. Sally can finish Uni and if we want to move somewhere else after that, we can.

Sally was the first to speak. 'I'd love to do that. I was a bit worried about being back in the city on my own now you've all finished.' She smiled shyly.

I grabbed her hand. 'We can all be together. What do you say ladies?'

Marianne and Laura agreed at once and the decision was made, Marianne would move north from London and a plan was made to look for somewhere to live before Sally's final year began.

'Raptio.' Said Sally to Miriam and Jeremy. 'That's what we're calling ourselves. What do you think?'

Her mother looked at her. 'That's a strange name darling, are you sure?'

Her father just smiled. 'Rapture, I like it.'

We all smiled at each other. It was agreed, we would be Raptio. If anyone else knew the other meanings of the word, they never said and we never bothered to explain it, other than to say it meant 'Rapture'.

'We can always change it to 'four musicians and a secret' if we're a complete flop.' I laughed later. 'Rising from the dead like a phoenix is what all the best rock stars do, they reinvent themselves regularly.'

The following weeks were busy with practice, arguments over playlists and finding somewhere to live. Favourite pieces were discussed endlessly and reworked to fit our quartet until we had a repertoire we were all happy with.

By the end of the holidays, we also had our first booking. A local wedding. A friend of Sally's accepted her offer of playing in lieu of a wedding present. Just twenty minutes as the evening guests were arriving, but it was enough to get three more enquiries for weddings later the same year.

We were on our way.

CHAPTER TWENTY-FIVE

I glanced at my watch. Jamie was late. Again!

Glancing down the street in the vain hope I would see him running to meet me I spotted a familiar figure.

Hunkered down in his coat, collar turned up against the rain he stood, watching me as I watched him.

Looking him over I realised the years had not been kind to Mr Smithson. Thoughtfully, I compared him to the confident, graceful man I had met at fourteen. Tramp-like was the best description I could give of him these days. I almost felt pity for him.

He turned away, as if he could read my thoughts and realised he had been found wanting. Scuttling into a side street, he was gone.

I wondered what had frightened him off and then, when a hand descended on my shoulder, I realised he must have seen Jamie approaching long before he arrived.

'I'm so sorry I'm late darling.' He looked nervous.

I smiled giving him a quick kiss on the cheek. 'Don't worry Jamie, I know you were probably up to something important. What was it this time?'

He grasped my hand tightly. 'I'll tell you when we get inside the restaurant.' And he guided me gently to the door.

'Mr Jamie, Miss Jenny, how nice to see you again.' Giorgio was effusive, we were his favourite customers, Raptio's impromptu recitals always went down well with his other guests.

We both smiled. 'Hello Giorgio, it's good to see you too.'

'Your usual table?' He asked. We nodded.

We had been eating here regularly for years and felt it was 'our' place as much as Giorgio's.

Settling in the booth, Giorgio bustled around, setting napkins on laps and fussing with the cutlery. When he left to get our drinks, Jamie grasped my hand again.

'Hello properly.' He was smiling broadly at me.

I laughed. 'Hello properly back.' So, you were going to tell me what kept you this time?'

'All in good time Jennifer, all in good time.' He loosened his grip on my hand as Georgio set down our drinks.

'Thanks, Giorgio.' I grinned at him as he winked conspiratorially at me and patted my head. 'Pizza?' He enquired about our usual order and Jamie nodded.

'He was here you know, outside; on the other side of the street, watching me.'

Jamie's face darkened. 'I'll bet he disappeared when I came along.'

I nodded. 'He must have seen you long before I did. He's changed, I realised it tonight. He's nothing like the man I remember, I almost felt sorry for him.' I patted Jamie's other hand to stop him before he got angry. 'It's ok, I don't feel sorry for him, far from it. But I had the feeling the years, the horrors, this game of cat and mouse has taken its toll on him, whilst we're thriving.' I was thoughtful for a moment. 'I feel a bit like a vampire, sucking the life force out of him. The stronger we become. Do you know what I mean?'

Jamie was forced to admit that all four women had grown over the years. All were accomplished and sought-after musicians in their own right, and they had never let the past define them. In fact, if he thought about it closely, it was those experiences which had made them who they were.

'Sort of, I think anyway.' He smiled thinly. 'But we did promise that none of you would ever be alone where something could happen and I apologise for putting you in that position tonight by being late.'

'It's ok Jamie.' I soothed him. 'For the first time, I wasn't frightened of him. Anyway, it's a busy high street, if he'd started to come over to me, I'd have come into Giorgio. It's funny isn't it that we keep seeing him pop up all over the place? He must live locally and yet we've never been able to track him down.'

Jamie nodded as I carried on. 'I feel like we're coming to the end of the game and we're on the winning team. Regardless of whether the police continue their investigations or not I know our plan is working, I only had to look at his face today to see he knew we were winning too.'

We had just started eating when Sally turned up with Marianne in tow.

'Hello you two, we wondered if you'd be here so thought we'd pop in.' Sally said, 'Hello Giorgio, any chance of squeezing in with Jamie and Jenny?'

Giorgio nodded and they budged up the seat.

A couple of minutes later, Laura and Davey joined us as well. 'Hi Giorgio can we grab a couple of chairs and join this miserable lot?' Davey laughed.

Giorgio obliged, bringing a chair for either end of the booth.

I was curious. 'What are you lot doing here? I thought we weren't doing anything until the weekend?'

Marianne picked at the bowl of olives in the middle of the table and Sally nibbled the end of a breadstick. 'Hey, those are our snacks, get your own.' Jamie admonished.

Laughing, Laura joined Sally in a breadstick. 'Make me.' She taunted waving the breadstick like a sword in his face until he laughed.

'Oh go on then, you're all obviously starving aren't you? I mean look at you, positively skin and bones, the lot of you.'

Davey patted his belly. 'It's all paid for Brother dearest.'

'You still haven't answered my question.' I complained.

A look from Jamie quieted me. He reached across to hold my hand. 'I was late tonight because I was collecting this.' His other hand drew a small box out of his pocket, and he placed it in front of my plate.

I looked at the box, confusion must have played across my face as the others all laughed. Then realisation dawned. 'Oh!'

I slowly opened the box and against the black velvet nestled a delicately beautiful emerald ring studded with tiny diamonds.

My hand flew to my mouth, I could hardly breathe. 'Jamie, it's beautiful.'

'It was my great-grandmother's, my grandmother's and my mother's engagement ring. Jennifer Hunter, will you marry me?'

I looked at him mutely for a moment and then nodded vigorously. 'Yes Jamie, yes I will.'

The others cheered. 'She said yes, she said yes.'

Davey called out 'Giorgio we need that champagne now please and don't forget your own glass too, you have to join the celebration because she said yes.'

Grinning Giorgio opened the bottle with a flourish, the cork sailing over the heads of the other diners who laughed and clapped along with our own small group in the corner.

Our wedding the following year was a lavish affair and one of North Norfolk's essential events of the season. My parents, Elizabeth and Jonathan went big inviting everyone we knew. I was after all, their only child.

For Jamie and I, the new Mr and Mrs de Tarbour, it passed in a whirl of guests, music, food and drink.

Kicking off my shoes towards the end of the evening, I sat down with my three best friends and bridesmaids.

'Whatever you do ladies; never, never get married.' I said darkly.

'But you look like you've had such fun.' Teased Laura in her best posh accent as she smoothed the front of the peach silk.

I thumped her on the shoulder. 'You don't honestly think this is 'fun' do you? Seriously, anything less 'fun like' I can't imagine. All those relatives I didn't know I had who popped out of the woodwork is enough to make me want to crawl into the nearest mouse hole.'

The others laughed. 'You've loved every minute of it and don't try to tell us otherwise. Miss 'I'm the centre of attention Jennifer Hunter .. oops correct that to de Tarbour'. Said Marianne.

I couldn't help smiling broadly as I watched my brand-new husband flirting with a couple of old aunts on the dance floor. 'He is rather wonderful isn't he.' I sighed dreamily.

'Where are you going for your honeymoon? Has Jamie told you yet?' Sally asked.

'I won't know until we get to the airport. Jamie even packed my suitcase for me before he left the house yesterday. Because I was with Mum and Dad, I have no idea what's missing from my wardrobe so can't even guess.' I flung my hands up in mock despair. 'I just hope, I've got the right shoes and enough jumpers.'

They all laughed at me.

'And what is my lovely wife laughing at now pray.' Jamie sat down and slipped an arm around my waist.

'We were just wondering if you'd packed enough knickers for the honeymoon.' Laughed Laura.

Jamie looked at her archly. 'She won't need knickers, will she? I thought the whole point of a honeymoon was to get out of our clothes and stay out of them as long as possible.'

He grinned when I slapped his leg.

'I'm not planning on staying in bed the whole time Mr de Tarbour, it might be nice to come up for air or a little excursion on the odd occasion. And besides we will have to eat.' I batted my eyes at him until he laughed again.

Our sex life had progressed more satisfactorily since we'd become engaged. It was almost as if seeing Mr Smithson as an object of pity rather than a dark power, had been the catalyst I needed to fully embrace my sexuality and love for Jamie.

Marianne interrupted my reverie. 'We have a gift for you both. I know you said 'no gifts' from us, but we couldn't let the occasion pass without something to mark the occasion. Jamie, it's more a gift for Jenny than you though.'

Signalling one of the waiters near the door she asked if he would bring in the box that was in reception.

A small box, beautifully wrapped, was delivered to our table. Marianne placed it in my hands saying. 'You might prefer to open this when you get to your room tonight rather than here in public.'

I must have looked quizzical. 'Can't I just take a peek inside?' And made as if to open it.

Sally slapped my hands away. 'We said no Jenny it's private and you'll just have to wait and, in the meantime, here's your father for the dance you promised him.'

The gift was whisked away, and I was pulled up gently by my father and into a waltz.

'Have you had a good day darling?' He asked.

'It's been fabulous Daddy, thank you so much. Jamie and I couldn't have asked for more support and help from you and mummy.' I hugged him hard and he returned the compliment.

'Your mother would like to have a chat before you go, make sure you see her.' he instructed.

'I will daddy, don't worry.' I assured him.

The dance ended and I found myself swept into the arms of my new father-in-law. Jeremy whirled me confidently around the dance floor, proud to show off the newest member of his family. When it ended, he bowed and handed me back to my new husband. 'Be happy Jennifer, you are a very welcome member of the family.' I smiled at him and then at Jamie before I was gathered up by friends and family for the rest of the evening.

The final dance of the evening was with my husband, Jamie. We spun and twirled for the guests who were on their feet clapping and laughing. I couldn't imagine being any happier than I was at the moment. It was perfect, life was perfect.

To leave the reception we had to pass through a long avenue of guests, all of whom wanted to have a few minutes of grace in our gilded circle. It took almost thirty minutes to make it through the compliments, the questions, and the suggestions. At the head of the avenue stood our families and closest friends.

I spoke quietly to my mother.

'Mummy, you've been amazing, thank you for everything, it's been the most magical day of my life and it wouldn't have been possible without you and daddy.' I hugged her, hard.

My mother pushed me back so she could look at me seriously. 'I am so proud of you Jennifer and you have such a lovely husband.' She smiled over at Jamie. 'Don't do anything to let him, or yourself down. I know things haven't been easy, and Daddy and I have never interfered, never asked as we know you'll tell us when you are ready. I hope that's still the case darling?'

Tears pricked my eyes, and I hugged her even harder. 'We will both tell you when we're ready. I love you so much Mummy.'

'And daddy and I both love you very much too darling. We want you to be happy and are looking forward to seeing you as the new Mr and Mrs de Tarbour when you get back from your honeymoon.' She released me to the rest of the little group.

Crowding around all our friends patted Jamie on the back and hugged me, in turn. With cries of 'wish we were there' and 'send a postcard' we were sent on our way to the honeymoon suite'.

Pushing the door open, I was amazed at the sea of flowers and a bottle of champagne in a bucket on the side table. And there was the gift box Marianne had so tantalisingly given and then swept away again. I picked it up and opened it slowly, nestled inside on cream paper was a beautiful broach of four roses, one for each of us. Four delicate silver stems and rose petals with a ruby, yellow emerald, garnet, and a black pearl at their heart bound together with a gold thread. It took my breath away

'Look.' I showed it to Jamie.

'It's gorgeous and the workmanship is outstanding, but is it something you want to wear? After all, it's a reminder of what's been happening over the years.'

I stood for a moment. 'No, actually it's perfect. It's a sort of full-stop. I said last year, we're coming to the end of the game, and this is the perfect way to celebrate, although I know that must sound odd.'

I walked over to where he was sitting on the bed and he caught my wrist, pulling me to him gently.

'How do you get this dress off?' He was impatiently pulling at the sleeves.

It was tightly fitted so I turned around so he could undo tiny seed pearl buttons running the length of the back one at a time.

'It was amazing.' I was keen to share every moment with my best friends when we gathered together for our first coffee following the honeymoon.

'And thank you for the broach, it was the perfect gift.' I pushed back my hair to make sure they could see it pinned on my jacket.

'We weren't sure how you would feel about it, but it seemed like the best way to show how strongly we are all connected.' Marianne was careful to include everyone in her glance.

I laughed. 'It was perfect and you couldn't have chosen better, although Jamie did say something about an electric carving knife being a bit more practical.'

They laughed and we carried on talking about the honeymoon.

'The sky was a blue I've only ever seen in a child's painting and the sea was so clear it sparkled and warm like stepping into a bath, completely unlike heading out for a swim in Dorset.' I laughed. 'We ate ourselves stupid every day, drank a little; it was just too hot for alcohol, slept and walked the beaches.' I sighed and sat back against the seat as I relived the memories of long lazy days and nights.

'And ….?' Laura encouraged.

'And .. what?' I asked with a grin.

Frustrated, Laura pushed her off her seat. 'You know, you and Jamie … was it all … you know … ok?'

Sally screwed up her face. 'Yuck, I don't want to know the details of what happens in my brother's sex life thank you very much.'

I smiled putting her out of her misery. 'It was better than ok Laura, but that's as far as I'm going with the details Sal.'

Marianne looked thoughtful. 'Maybe there's hope for the rest of us yet then.' She spoke quietly and looked away.

'Speak for yourself, Marianne. Davey and I are just fine thanks very much.' Shared Laura.

Sally screwed up her face again. 'Ladies, they are my brothers, please. I really do not want to know.' She looked at Marianne. 'You and I should do something, how about a dating agency?' She offered.

Marianne shook her head. 'No thanks, Sally. It reminds me of a cattle market, and I'm not ready to be poked and prodded just yet thanks.'

I joined in. 'You two never go anywhere without us.' I held up my hand as they started to protest. 'It's true, you don't. So, perhaps that's the place to start.' I hoped my tone would brook no argument and they nodded meekly.

'Perhaps you're right.' Sighed Marianne. 'It's been so long since I swore off men that I stopped thinking about it at all.' She picked up my left hand. 'It's only since you got married that I've begun to wonder what I might be missing out on.'

Sally nodded in agreement. 'I might be the youngest of the group, but I've never really met anyone I would want to tell my story to.' She looked down. 'I'm always worried they might do what my school friends did and back off, thinking it was my fault.'

Laura's face softened. 'First, you have to want to. And it sounds like you've both got to that point finally.' She looked around the pub and began pointing out suitable men until we were all in stitches and the tension had broken.

CHAPTER TWENTY-SIX

Our next performance took place the following Saturday evening. The venue, a large auditorium, had been booked to accommodate the extensive fan base we had gathered over our years of playing together.

It was our first large-scale privately managed event and we all experienced that thrilling mixture of nervous anticipation tinged with excitement and happiness.

Gathering in the dressing room, we were comparing notes when the roses arrived. We all looked at each other. It was Laura who broke the silence.

'Just how many of these have we received over the years, a few dozen each?' She frowned trying to remember.

I smiled and looked at my broach. It was my good luck charm, and I wore it at every performance.

Over the years, we had tried to give the roses to the police, but they weren't 'evidence' of anything. Their indifference had led to us closing ranks.

Laura continued. 'Don't you think it's odd he sends them when he comes and that we don't get them when he doesn't?'

We looked at her wondering where she was going.

'Well, there's a pattern of sorts to it, don't you think'. She finished lamely.

I nodded in agreement. 'You're right Laura, remember years ago when I explained that plan to you? Well, I've been keeping notes all this time and there is a pattern, it's not fully clear yet, but the roses are definitely a part of it.'

Marianne hesitated. 'When you said you had a plan you also said you were going to kill him.'

I looked at her. 'I never actually said I would kill him, I think you'll find I just said, "kill him", nothing more or less than that.'

'And there's a difference?' Sally's voice rose with the question.

I nodded. 'There is indeed a difference Sal, but I'm not ready to tell you yet.' I held out my hands to them all. 'Is that ok?'

Laura grasped my hand back. 'Knowing you're on the case is good enough for me.' She looked at the other two willing them to agree.

They nodded as well. 'We'll wait.' said Marianne.

'It won't be long now.' I promised. 'But we are going to move things up a gear'. And instead of dumping the roses in the bin I put them in a vase and took them with us to the stage. It was time to let Mr Smithson know that we were in control now.

Two years further on we found ourselves enjoying one of those rare days you sometimes get in Winter, the ones with blue skies and a warmth that held the promise of Summer. The only thing missing from the scene was the tree's green lacey dresses; even the insects were out in force.

I walked rapidly along the cliff top, deep in thought. Images of actions taken flashed rapidly through my head as I mentally ticked off the 'to-do' list I'd prepared.

We were playing for charity to a packed house of hand-picked guests. The people we had 'invited' to buy tickets were all either known to a member of our families, were old friends or colleagues.

Despite the posters, the adverts, the radio, and television interviews we had each given to publicise the event; there was only one ticket actually for sale to a member of the public. We didn't know but were hopeful it had been picked up by the right person.

Even the ticket agency had been fabricated using a post office box in Exeter for cover.

The cheques and payments came from far and wide; those we were expecting were approved and the tickets dispatched; those we didn't know were put to one side. We were looking for one special application, one special person.

When it came, Jamie had punched the air, his face grim. 'We've nailed him'.

I urged him to caution. 'We think it's him, we can't be sure Jamie; remember that.'

He'd grabbed my hands. 'I just know it; I just know this is him.'

A single ticket, paid for with cash and sent by recorded delivery with a return address of another post office box in Leeds. 'People just don't do things like that these days.' His explanation was eminently reasonable.

The application was approved. The ticket was dispatched. The trap was set.

I looked at the rose nestled in its box in my hand. I remember I was shaking slightly and felt sick. I was going to finish, finally, what had started in a quiet music room twelve years earlier.

I thought of my friends, my fellow members of our small ensemble and wondered how they would be feeling, now the day had arrived, and the plan looked like it might just work.

Five years in the making, it felt like a lifetime had been lived already. Each year's passing is marked with more information gathered.

It had been an off-the cuff remark from Laura, at university, that had me thinking along the tracks we had all followed so carefully, never straying once from the agreed actions, never once taking a chance that might expose what we were planning.

Mr Smithson, or whomever he was, didn't attend all her performances, just some. As far as I was concerned, that meant one of two things; either another life was getting in the way, or what she was playing wasn't to his taste.

I took a chance that it was the latter, a chance time proved had almost certainly been right.

Since we began playing together I had kept detailed notes of our repertoire, what we wore, the location, the size of the audience and the type of venue. All these years later I had the evidence in my hand.

The roses were only delivered when he was in the audience. He would choose a seat that allowed one of our number to see him clearly from the stage but he would be out of sight of the others. When no roses arrived, we could be reasonably sure he wasn't there. Of course, we might all have been playing an imaginary game of chess, without realising we had an opponent, but that was not what my instinct told me.

It was as if he got some morbid, curious satisfaction thinking that one of us was going to be discomforted. It reminded me horribly, of the lessons in self-discipline I had mastered all those years ago. There was no doubt about it, he had taught me well. Apart from feeling dread when the roses arrived, our performances were always flawless.

I sometimes wondered if, in his mind, he was simply continuing the lessons.

Of course, we'd asked friends and family to be at our performances over the years; to watch with Jamie and Davey the entrances and exits, just in case someone could catch him. But he had a cat-like ability to enter and leave the smallest of buildings with ease and had never been spotted.

When we talked it over, we came up with all sorts of theories, the most likely was a disguise of some sort.

He had never looked a particular age. To me he had been in his mid-twenties; to Marianne, he was older than that by several years, and she had been his first. I realised that when I spotted him in London and at St Cecilia's, all those years ago.

So, we were forced to take drastic action. As Jamie said, the sick charade had to stop, and tonight, if everything went to plan, it would stop, dead!

We wore dresses to match our rose colour. Sally's was the brightest canary yellow, Marianne's a deep burgundy that set off her dark colouring to perfection. Laura wore a delicate pink, barely there at all. And of course, I was in black, full length and with a deep décolletage.

We looked confident, poised, and beautiful.

The setting of our final performance for Mr Smithson was an intimate village hall in Dorset, near the cliffs and the sea. Jamie and Davey, as usual, were watching the entrances, but by the time the audience was seated had to admit they didn't know where he had chosen to sit.

It wasn't his usual choice for a performance, probably because of the risks associated with the size of the venue.

But, the lure, of the pieces we were playing had, as it turned out and as we hoped, proved too much for him to ignore.

The roses had arrived, we knew he was there, somewhere.

Unbeknownst to Mr Smithson, a member of every family, someone who could recognise their members of the audience, had been drafted in unwittingly to help identify his car and the owner.

Keeping them outside, Jamie and Davey held them in conversation until the performance was due to start, paying careful attention to the cars coming in and the subsequent greetings with their captives. Their assumption was he would be the only member of the audience not to be greeted as a friend, relation or acquaintance. The assumption proved flawed; however, it didn't matter. Everyone else who went by unacknowledged was in couples.

Just one person arrived alone, parking his convertible in the corner of the car park.

He walked confidently to the door, handed his ticket to the usher, bought a programme, and picked up a leaflet about the charity we were supporting.

Jamie and Davey retrieved the ticket and scanned it under the infrared torch.

This time it was Davey's turn to punch the air.

The ticket had been marked with an invisible marker.

It was him.

We began with Debussy, passed through Telemann and Mozart and Bach, and ended with Pachelbel. It was the perfect recital set. It was the perfect trap. The net was closing in.

The evening ended and the applause was long and strong, not one member of the audience moved until we had left the stage; and when they did, it was slowly, in drips and drabs, small groups and pairs.

By the time we left the hall, the car park had emptied to just one car beside our own. It was stuck in the corner with a flat tyre, helped along by the glass shard which Jamie just happened to have to hand.

I squeezed Jamie's hand as Laura gave Davey a quick kiss.

Looking at the others, we nodded in agreement. It was time to complete the tick box on my 'to-do' list.

The hall had been chosen for its location.

Far enough away from the town to need a car to get there, but not so far you couldn't walk if you happened to need help with a flat tyre. There was no phonebox until you reached the next village a couple of miles west, and the only route was over the cliffs. It was a path we knew well from the many summers spent in Dorset.

Clothed warmly in jeans, boots, and dark jackets, we set off with Sally leading the way. She knew the clifftop path best of all and we didn't want any accidents.

It didn't take long for the lights of the village hall to die away to nothing. We'd chosen the night well, hoping that a full moon would work in our favour, banking on fine weather. Although the dark was encompassing, we could still see reasonably well.

Sure of our steps, knowing where the ruts, gulley's and potholes were meant we could walk briskly, far more quickly than if you'd never walked the path before.

Someone like that would stumble and feel their way in the dark.

And it wasn't long before we caught up with him. At the highest point on the path.

We were young, healthy, and fit. He was old, overweight, and frightened.

'Mr Smithson.' I called. He stopped, shook his head as if he was hearing things and then carried on walking.

'Mr Johnson.' Called Laura. He stopped again, turned around and seeing his four girls smiled nervously.

'You gave a marvellous performance tonight.' He started.

No one replied, we hadn't come for chit-chat.

We walked towards him slowly, in a line that started to circle round the sides of him, pushing him in the direction we wanted.

He took a step back involuntarily, holding his hands up as if to defend himself from an imaginary assailant.

We carried on walking. Staring at him. I could hear my friends breathing heavily and the thump of their boots. My senses, and theirs I assumed, had been heightened. The cold frosted my fingertips, and I could feel a buzz in my belly, nerves I supposed. I had never felt so alive and focused.

'What do you want?' The fear in his voice was palpable.

The agreement had been that we would not speak. Speaking was a danger, it would allow the man we had all known a back door into our minds. We couldn't afford to let that happen.

We stared at him and carried on walking towards him, herding him towards the cliff edge.

He stumbled and fell onto one knee.

'Ladies, please. Just tell me what you want, and I'll try to make it better.' The tables had turned. No longer were we the mice and he the cat. You could feel it in the air, the past was being rewritten.

We carried on walking, pushing him towards the destination we had in mind, a loose semi-circle enclosing him.

His look was like a frightened rabbit, caught in the headlights. At that moment, I knew any power he had over us had been diminished, was gone. The power was in our hands, and we were the ones who were teaching him valuable life lessons now.

I checked the position of the others, there was nowhere to run to except through us and we were close enough to trip him up should he try.

'Do you hate me that much?' He pleaded. 'We looked at him, stunned he could even ask such a question.

'Look what I gave you?' He tried a different tack.

Gave us? I was incredulous. What he gave us was a decade and more of hell. Of coping with our internal demons which pinned the blame fairly and squarely on our young shoulders. Shoulders which should have been free of heavy weights.

I opened my mouth to speak, ready to break our promise not to say anything, no matter how provoked we were. A glance from Marianne silenced me and I closed my mouth again.

Instead, I cocked my head to one side and put a questioning expression on my face, mimicking one he had used with me frequently when I wasn't quite on track with the music, or the dance.

'Without me, you'd be nothing. All of you.' He spat the words out, hoping to delay the inevitable.

We just carried on looking at him.

'You know that you all had to be taught to fight for your music, fight for your life, fight as if it was the only thing that mattered.' He was ranting now and it was clear he genuinely believed he had done us a great service.

He carried on. 'Without me, none of you would be where you are now. You would not be feted and applauded. You would not be booked by the best venues. You would not be famous.' He shot the last words out of his mouth like a slingshot hoping to wound. We were unmoved.

I reflected that in many ways he was probably right. Without that 'training' as he called it Laura, and I, would definitely not be the musicians we were. We could cope with anything. But my thoughts brought me back to Sally and Marianne, what about them? How had his rape of their youth and innocence benefited them?

The question must have shown on my face, or I might have looked at them standing near each other, because he turned to look at them too.

'My beautiful one and My sweetest one'. He spoke quietly, just to them, almost out of earshot. 'You were my regrets. I wish I had had longer with you both, teaching you the ways of music in a more structured and enjoyable way.' He sighed and looked at me. 'You, Jennifer Hunter' he used my maiden name deliberately. 'You were my beloved, but you left me.' He cried plaintively. 'You left me alone and with nowhere to turn. If you hadn't done what you did, I would have had no need to look for ease elsewhere. I would never have punished my sweetest one for your wrongdoing.'

Laura caught my arm before I said anything.

'You were the one I wanted, always. You were the one I've been waiting for, to come home to me; to come back to me. Will you come back to me Jennifer Hunter? Will you?'

I turned away, disgusted, he hadn't said anything I hadn't thought for myself over the years. If only I had been less naïve, then perhaps Laura and Sally could have been spared the ordeal they endured.

I looked up and saw Sally smiling at me, shaking her head as if to tell me to rid that image from my head. I turned to look at Laura and she did the same. She smiled and grabbed my hand, holding it tightly, as if to say, 'It's not your fault.' I was grateful to both of them and hoped my eyes conveyed that thought.

Turning back, we walked a step closer, pushing him further along, even closer to the cliff edge.

Looking back, he wobbled when he realised just how close he was. We watched a stain creep down his trousers as he peed himself. Fear was his friend now. We had successfully passed it back to where it belonged.

A small voice, seeming to come from nowhere, could be heard in the group. 'I'm sorry.'

This was what we wanted, this is what we'd been pushing for, this was the moment to clarify.

I spoke clearly. 'What are you sorry for Mr Smithson or Mr Johnson, whoever you are?'

He looked down, defeated. 'I don't want to meet my maker like this, I don't want to die, I'm not ready to die.' He dropped to his knees and grovelled. 'Please, don't do this, don't let me die here, now, with you all hating me.'

He looked up, straight into my eyes and I gazed back as impassively as I could, despite the roiling in my stomach, I wanted to be sick.

'I'm sorry I hurt you, I'm sorry I raped you, I'm sorry I abused you, I'm sorry.' He hung his head and wept.

We stood aside as the police crept out of the thick bracken and gorse surrounding us and arrested him. The victory felt hollow, and our shoulders sagged, the strain was too much and we all wept, using each other for support.

The policewoman assigned to our case came over. 'That was great girls, you did extremely well tonight.' She looked at me. 'It was a good plan Jenny, and you were right, we were wrong.'

The acknowledgement that they had been wrong was the catalyst for a fresh bout of crying. Having spent so many hours in various rooms with the police over the years, to finally have the acceptance that we were right was a hard-won triumph.

'What happens now?' Laura asked her.

'He'll be taken back to the station and charged with rape and indecent assault.' She spoke factually.

'Will he get bail?' Asked Sally.

'It's unlikely, the fact that he's stalked you for so long would put paid to that with any judge and the likelihood of him harming you or himself is probably quite high, so he'll be detained until his trial unless he pleads guilty.'

We all heaved a collective sigh of relief.

Sheila, our police liaison officer drove us home. As soon as I stepped through the doors, Jamie folded me in his arms. 'Is it done?'

I nodded and began to weep quietly. My parents joined Jamie and I as the other parents all emerged from the drawing room to see their daughters too.

'We need tea.' Said Miriam, calling for Peter.

Davey, his arm loosely around Laura's shoulder, said 'Shouldn't it be champagne?'

His mother shook her head. 'Tomorrow perhaps, but right now the girls are all in shock, even if they don't realise it. Tea, something to eat and bed is what they need.'

I was grateful for her intervention I started crying all over again and my mother and Jamie stroked my shoulders, soothing me.

The day had been long, all I wanted was to crawl into a bed, be wrapped in safety by my husband's arms, and sleep.

It took two days for the story to break in the newspapers. When it did it hit every headline from Dorset to the far northwest of Scotland. Major newspapers ran with the headline 'Is this the worst sex offender in Britain?' with a picture of his face staring out at us from every newsagent and newsstand.

There was an avalanche of others. The women whose lives he had touched came forward in their droves. The common factor? Yes, you've guessed it, they were all musicians when they were young.

Jamie and Davey noticed it first. 'They all look like you four, have you noticed?'

As it happens, we hadn't, but when we started paying attention to the emerging stories we could see a distinct resemblance both in instrument and looks; as if we were the mould he had cast everyone else on.

The police never did find out who he was. His fingerprints never matched anything recorded and he had never been arrested before. He had relied, it turned out, on the same flawed system which had defeated us so many times; that, and the guilt of the abused, the feeling that somehow it was all your fault.

The day he died dawned bright and clear.

He shared a cell with two other prisoners on remand and they had led him to believe he wouldn't make it out of there alive when he first arrived.

He hadn't slept properly since, waking at the slightest stirring of his companions.

Recreation was the opportunity he needed, everyone had disappeared off the wing and by the time the officers came looking, it was too late, the light had gone from his eyes; the laced-together arms of prison clothing had done their job effectively, even if he had kicked over the chair in his last spasms.

There was no note.

No note to tell the mother no one knew he was sorry, the sister he had long since lost touch with, or the father who watched the news and kept quiet about the son he would never admit to raising.

We were informed by our liaison officer, Sheila, who was probably not surprised to see little emotion flicker across our faces.

'What will you do now?' Laura asked.

Sheila looked confused. 'I'm not sure what you mean?'

'With the body, what will happen to his body?' Laura explained.

'It will be cremated as no one has come forward to claim him.' Sheila explained.

Laura paused for a moment, head cocked to one side. 'Will there be a funeral?'

Sheila nodded. 'Of sorts, at the crematorium. Why, would you like to go?'

Laura looked at each of us and we all nodded. 'Yes please.' She replied for all of us.

'I am the resurrection and the life. says the Lord. Those who believe in me, even though they die, will live, and everyone who lives and believes in me will never die.'

The minister intoned the words at the front of the chapel. We four placed our roses on his coffin and stepped back to join our families. There were no tears, no discreetly held hankies; there was a sense of an ending, a passing, and a resolution.

We were finally free.

FINALE

Jenny stepped lightly out of the taxi and looked up. She half expected to see Mr Smithson waiting for her and was surprised to note the slight disappointment she felt.

She shivered, it was April and should have been warming up, but the wind bit as it rushed round the corner of the magistrate's court.

'Are you ready darling?' Her father reached for her hand and she grasped it gratefully.

'As ready as I'll ever be Dad'. She smiled to show she was OK.

As they started up the steps, the notes of Pachelbel's Canon in D drifted through the open window of the marriage room. She smiled, it was her favourite and the one she'd always wanted for her wedding day.

'Do you remember learning to play that when you were just 14 Jenny?'

'I do' she smiled at her father. 'And I remember telling Mummy that it would be the music I got married to.'

Her father laughed, 'We always knew you'd had a rough day at school because that was the piece you turned to time and again. In fact, at one point I hid the score. By then though, you knew it so well you didn't need it.'

'I didn't realise you knew Dad.'

'No, we never said darling, just waited until you came to tell us in your own time.'

At the top of the steps, they turned left, away from the marriage room and towards the coroner's office. Outside, they met the others. And there was Jamie, the husband she had walked down the aisle to as Pachelbel's Canon in D played by her friends, her bridesmaids and the women she had shared so much of her life with.

He smiled. 'Feeling OK?'

She nodded. 'It's time to finish this, isn't it?' And walked into the hearing to hear the outcome.